MURDER ON A SPRING DAY

A light-hearted English whodunit mystery

JON HARRIS

Published by The Book Folks

London, 2024

© Jon Harris

ISBN 978-1-80462-147-9

www.thebookfolks.com

MURDER ON A SPRING DAY is the third novel in this addictive series of cozy English mysteries. Head to the back of this book for details about the other titles.

For Jeni

Chapter 1

Julia sat behind the counter of her bookshop. The opening rush had quietened down now. She wouldn't use the word 'bonanza', because it hadn't been one, but business in their first month had been brisk for them.

Them being her and her boyfriend Mark, who was leaning on the counter, complaining about his latest job. Although he'd been hanging around the shop, getting under her feet since 4.30 p.m. Any job which let out that early didn't seem like it could be quite so terrible to Julia.

He had white paint streaked across one cheek, something that Julia wondered if he did on purpose to be endearing. She was just considering wetting one finger and wiping the paint off when the shop door clattered open and a man came in, looking hurried. He was average height and middle-aged. His most outstanding feature was his suit, which even Julia could tell looked expensive and well-tailored.

If Julia was examining the man, then he was repaying the attention with interest, looking at her bug-eyed as he bustled across the shop floor to her.

"Are you Julia Ford?" the man asked, slightly breathless.

"Yes," Julia replied.

"The private detective?"

Julia opened her mouth to tell the man she was no such thing, but Mark spoke before she could.

"That's right," he said. "The private detective."

Julia glared daggers at Mark. It was true that she had, on a couple of occasions now, assisted the police in catching killers. But they had purely been a case of her being in the right place at the right time. Or looked at another way, the wrong place at the wrong time. Either way, a private investigator she wasn't.

However it seemed her look was completely lost on the newcomer. "Good," he said. "Because I need your help."

"What's the problem?" asked Mark.

The man began to speak but Julia quickly cut him off.

"We can't discuss this here in front of all the customers," she hissed to Mark.

One elbow still on the counter, Mark made a show of turning to look round at the shop floor, empty except for the three of them and the stacks of books.

To Julia's dismay, the stranger also looked round over their shoulder. When his head swivelled back to her, it bore a confused look.

"Well, there might be a last-minute rush," Julia said. She sighed and looked at the man. "I suppose that you might as well carry on."

The man extended his hand which she noticed was slightly damp when she shook it.

"My name is Ronald Cutty," he said. "I run an accounting firm over in King's Barrow. Cutty and Partners. You've probably heard of us."

Julia hadn't, but she nodded anyway.

"On Friday an employee of mine, Miss Beatrice Campbell was–" Mr Cutty swallowed, his Adam's apple rising and falling before he continued "–strangled to death."

"I heard about that," Julia said. "How awful."

In truth, when Julia had read in the papers that there had been a local murder, she'd felt a mild sense of relief that for once she wasn't caught up in the middle of it. Now she had a sinking feeling that was about to change.

"I know," Mr Cutty said. "But what's more is that the police seem to think that I was the one who did it."

"I take it you didn't," Mark said, less than helpfully in Julia's opinion.

"No. It's just a misunderstanding, that's all."

Julia could sympathize. She too had fallen foul of the police force's eagerness to pin a crime on an easy mark rather than follow all the leads.

"Why do they think it was you?" Julia asked.

Mr Cutty shifted uncomfortably, tugging at the cuffs of his suit jacket. "We had an argument in the office," he said. "I wasn't exactly pleased with some of the work that she'd done. It got rather heated, I'm afraid to say, and she ended up storming out. After work I went to her home."

"And you found her dead?" Mark finished for him.

"No," Mr Cutty said. "She was alive and well. Although not thrilled to see me. She threw a glass at me and I left. According to the time of death, she must have been killed shortly afterwards."

"I can see why the police would get the wrong idea," Julia said gently.

"I suppose so," replied Mr Cutty. "That and the fact she dialled 999 as she was dying and told the operator my name."

"She called the police while being strangled to death?" Mark asked.

"No, no," said Mr Cutty. "She was strangled with something. The cord from her kettle, I think. It was tied around her neck when she was found. Anyway, the police think she was left for dead and although she managed to make the call, it appears she wasn't able to untie the cord. At any rate she only managed one word on the call."

"That word being your name," said Julia. All of a sudden she felt slightly uneasy.

A frown creased up Mr Cutty's face. "Please don't look at me like that. I know how it sounds. I'd never harm a fly. But the police simply don't believe a word I tell them. That's why I came to you for help."

Julia exchanged a quick look with Mark. At least with him present she wasn't in any immediate danger. There wouldn't be any harm in at least looking into things.

A gentle tinkling filled the air as the door opened, setting the bell ringing.

Three heads as one turned and watched as Mrs Singh stepped into the room. She froze in the doorway, blinking, and gave them a puzzled look before sidling over to the baking section.

"Okay," Julia said, leaning in over the counter, speaking in a conspiratorial whisper. "I'll meet you after work and we'll discuss it further. You said Miss Campbell was killed in her home? We'll start there."

* * *

The atmosphere in Mark's van was decidedly frosty. They weren't driving in silence – the good people at Radio 5 Live saw to that – but neither of them was talking.

Not for the first time, Julia looked at Mark out of the corner of her eye as he drove. At her behest he'd gone back to her house to clean the paint off his face and change into some fresh clothes and generally not look like a complete disgrace in front of this person who was – and Julia couldn't believe she was referring to him as this – their client.

Apparently Mark could feel her watching. "I know you're not happy with me," he said.

Julia remained silent and turned her eyes to the road ahead. It was about half an hour's drive to the address that Mr Cutty had given them on the edge of King's Barrow.

Mark continued. "It is remarkable what you did though. Solving those murders the way you did when the police couldn't. Maybe you should be a private investigator, you know? If the shoe fits."

Julia made a little harrumph noise, but she could feel her resolve weakening. Early in their relationship Mark had figured out flattery was usually the fruitful approach with her.

"And besides," Mark said, "we could use the extra money."

That finally drew a response from Julia; her head swung round to look at him, mouth open. "We are not charging that man," she snapped.

"Why not?"

"Because he needs our help, Mark," said Julia.

"Of course he does. But private investigators still charge for their services, don't they?"

Julia grunted with annoyance. "We are not private investigators," she said. "I'm only helping Mr Cutty because I know just what it's like when the police go for the obvious suspect regardless of their innocence. It's not a nice feeling. I seem to remember that you weren't a lot of help at the time, either," she added.

The barb struck and Mark looked wounded. He drove on a bit further, taking an exit off the main road out of the rush hour traffic and onto one of the quieter streets. According to the satnav on his phone they were almost there now.

"So you're not planning on charging him?" Mark said.

"No," replied Julia.

Mark pouted. "Then who will buy me pretty things?" he asked.

Julia gave a martyred sigh. "You're pretty enough already," she said.

Mark reached over to give Julia's hand a squeeze but she batted it away. "Concentrate please, you're driving," she said.

Mark pulled the van to a halt and reached out again. "Not anymore," he said.

Julia batted his hand away again, more vigorously. "Stop fooling around, Mark. We'll be late meeting Mr Cutty."

"We're here," Mark said.

Julia squinted through the windscreen. They seemed to be in the car park of a frozen foods supermarket. A defunct one, by the look of the plyboard over the windows.

"This is where the satnav told me to go," Mark said.

Julia was about to lay into her other half's map-reading skills, which she had lost faith in after an ill-fated trip to Cornwall with his parents which had only been salvaged by thinking on the fly and turning it into a Cotswolds trip. But then she saw a car swinging into the car park next to them, Mr Cutty behind the wheel.

Mark didn't get a chance to say I told you so, as Julia quickly unbuckled and slipped out of the van.

Mr Cutty slammed his car door behind him, the sound echoing around the empty black space of the car park, and stepped forward to meet Julia.

"I'm sorry I'm a bit late," he said.

"No problem, Mr Cutty," Julia said.

"Please, call me Ronald."

"Okay, Ronald. And this is where Beatrice Campbell lives?" Julia asked, making a show of looking up and down the boarded-up frontage of the supermarket. Poorly executed graffiti covered most of the plyboards. A handful of small trees lined the front of it. Despite it being spring now, they had all failed to bud.

"Her flat's above the shop. I'll show you the way up," Mr Cutty said, gesturing to the side of the long, squat building.

Julia and Mark followed as he led the way past the empty trolley park, litter lifting up in swirls on the breeze as they went.

"Tell us again why you were here the night Miss Campbell was murdered," Julia said.

"It started in my office," Mr Cutty replied. "I had some issues with some of the work Beatrice had done. We both let emotion rather run away with us, I'm afraid. She stormed off home, causing a bit of a scene. When work had finished and I'd calmed down, I drove over to see if I could do anything to salvage the situation. Well, it turned out that she hadn't done much calming down. As soon as she answered the door to me, she was raging. She had a glass in her hand and she threw it at me."

Mr Cutty raised his right hand up to show Julia. It was hard to make out with the only light coming from a stand of streetlights in the centre of the car park, some two hundred feet away. But she could see a curved mark across his palm. From what he was saying, Julia gathered it must be a cut from the glass.

They reached the end of the building and rounded the corner. As they did so, a bright white security light overhead blinked on, causing Julia to squint. Rather incongruously, a simple white front door was set into the wall underneath it.

It was a very plain-looking white door, with no number on it and a slightly rusty letter box set into it. Two strands of police tape hung limply across the frame around chest height.

The first thing Julia noticed was that the frame around the handle had been staved in. The frame was thick and sturdy, it looked like breaking it would have taken some doing.

She pointed to it. "Was it the killer who did this?"

Mr Cutty shook his head. "The police, when they responded to the 999 call."

He pointed his own finger, drawing Julia's attention to a small glass protrusion on the door around eye height, which she had taken as a peephole.

"This is a camera for a JeevesDoor," he said.

"JeevesDoor?" Julia asked.

"One of those camera doorbells," Mr Cutty explained. "Whenever someone presses the doorbell, it takes a photo and sends it to your phone so you can see who it is. That's how the police know that I was here. They have my photo from when I called in on her. Apparently I was the last person to do so." He glanced at the police tape barring their way. "I suppose this is all I can show you really."

Mark reached one of his long arms between the two of them and raised the tape up.

"Don't worry, Ronald," he said. "We're allowed, we're PIs."

"Oh, I didn't know that," Mr Cutty replied, as he ducked his head under and stepped through the doorway.

Julia looked at Mr Cutty as he disappeared inside, flicking the light on as he did so. Then she turned and looked meaningfully at Mark and sighed. "We'd better make this quick then," she said.

"Why's that?" Mark still had his arm raised, holding up the tape.

"Well what if the actual police arrive?" she hissed, struggling to keep her voice down. "Then we'd be in trouble."

"Unless it was my dad," said Mark.

"I think we'd still be in trouble."

Mark gave a little shrug. "I'm used to being in trouble with him."

Julia didn't have time to argue, so she stepped through under the tape and into Beatrice's flat, Mark sliding in behind her.

Immediately inside the doorway, a set of stairs led up over the supermarket. The stairs were steep, covered only in a threadbare carpet and smelled faintly of mildew. At the top was a second door, a regular interior door, which Mr Cutty was just opening as Julia reached the top of the stairs.

The second door led into the flat, which was less spartan and depressing than the entryway had been, although that was setting rather a low bar.

Julia cast a glance back down the stairs. That at least answered her first question before she even needed to ask it. Anyone wanting to let Beatrice know they were there would have to use the doorbell. Knocking on the front door to make yourself known would have been fairly futile, unless you were going to cause an absolute ruckus pounding on it.

"Careful where you tread," Mr Cutty warned, as Julia followed him inside.

A jumble of broken glass littered the carpet just inside the doorway. The various pieces were just recognizable as the remains of a drinking tumbler.

"Whatever happened, it must have been soon after you left," Julia said as she edged around them. "It seems Beatrice didn't get a chance to tidy it up."

"Based on the time of the 999 call, it was only a few minutes after I drove off," Mr Cutty said. He sighed and pushed open the door to the kitchen. "This is where they found her body," he added.

Julia wasn't quite sure what she'd been expecting. Maybe the chalk outline of a figure, sprawled dramatically on the floor. Instead there was just a couple of small bits of yellow plastic with numbers on to mark out points of interest.

She stepped cautiously over the top of one of them and took a look around. The linoleum tiles were illuminated evenly by the half-dozen or so spotlights in the ceiling. There were a few signs of the struggle that had taken place there.

The kettle lay on its side on one of the counters. The cord to plug it in was missing. Mr Cutty had said it was the murder weapon so presumably the police had taken it as evidence.

The phone, fixed to the wall next to the humming refrigerator, was hanging off by its long cord, dangling limply just above the floor.

There was a square, pine two-seater table against the opposite wall. One of the chairs had been upended, apparently with some force since there were grooves gouged into the floor where it had landed.

Julia crossed the room and looked out of the window. All that greeted her was a bleak view out over the car park and the jagged railing of the security fence beyond it.

"Are there any other ways into the flat?" she asked. "Ways that meant Beatrice wouldn't have opened the front door?"

"No other doors, just the windows," Mr Cutty said. "The police tell me that they were all locked shut when they arrived at the scene."

Mark was making his own circuit of the kitchen and looked down at the catch on the window nearest to him. "I suppose someone could have come in through one of the windows, locked it behind them, and left through the door," he said.

"That's what I suggested to the police, but they weren't interested." Mr Cutty sniffed and Julia once more felt a pang of sympathy for him.

But peering down at the sheer drop to the front of the shop, Julia reckoned that if someone had come in through a window they would have to be pretty athletic. "Or Beatrice might have known they were coming and let them in," she said. "Then they wouldn't have rung the doorbell."

"If she knew they were coming then it would suggest the crime was personal," Mark added.

"I'm told it's unlikely." Mr Cutty sounded disdainful though. Another line of thought he'd hashed over with the police. "Her mobile was completely dead and hadn't been on for over a day. At least it hadn't pinged a tower."

"Would she even have known people were ringing the doorbell then, if her phone was dead?" Mark asked.

"The doorbell still rings in the flat even if her phone's dead," said Mr Cutty.

"I don't think I could function without my phone for over a day," Julia mused.

"Well there's the landline," Mr Cutty said, and he nodded to where the receiver hung by its cord, swaying gently from their movements about the room. "But the police said there hadn't been any calls on it on the day of her murder. Not until, well, you know…"

Mr Cutty trailed off. He'd already told them that Beatrice had managed to dial 999 after the attack and then said his name. Julia made a mental note to get her hands on that 999 recording.

Her eyes moved from the phone to the spot on the floor where Beatrice had taken her last breath, which was marked by a simple yellow plastic token. Strangled. Julia couldn't think of a more horrible thing. She shuddered. The attack seemed like it was a very personal crime. Not the sort of thing she could imagine a burglar doing if they got disturbed and panicked.

"Do you know if Beatrice had anyone who would want to hurt her?" Julia asked.

"Oh yes, lots." Mr Cutty nodded thoughtfully, chewing on his bottom lip.

Julia and Mark both turned to look at him, but he stood with his hand in the pockets of his suit trousers, looking down at the marker on the floor.

"Please, go on," Mark prompted.

"Well she was embezzling money from her clients, you see," Mr Cutty said.

Julia blinked. "All of them?" she asked.

Mr Cutty shrugged his shoulders. "That's what we're working with the police to determine now. Some of them at least. That's what the argument at work was about. One of her clients raised irregularities to me. That was the first we knew of it, but it's possible that another victim had realized as well."

Julia exchanged a look with Mark. At least it didn't seem as though they were going to be short of suspects.

"Did she admit the embezzlement?" Mark asked.

"No," Mr Cutty replied. "She was furious with me for suggesting it. But the client, that's the parish council by the way, well, the evidence they presented was pretty clear-cut. Her figures weren't adding up in the slightest. You see, what we think she was doing…"

Julia nodded politely as Mr Cutty expounded on the details of Beatrice's scheme. After a few minutes she could feel her eyes glazing over and forced herself to pay attention. It all seemed dazzlingly complicated.

"…All rather simple really, I suppose," Mr Cutty concluded.

Mark gave a slight cough. "Yes," he said.

Julia doubted he'd followed the intricacies any better than she had. At any rate money had gone missing from the accounts Beatrice Campbell managed. In rather large quantities. That seemed to be the salient part.

"Do you think you'll be able to help?" Mr Cutty asked, his voice full of hope.

"We can look into it," said Julia, "starting with the parish council. We'll see if they might have taken matters into their own hands." She might not know how the embezzlement had worked, but solving murders she was all too familiar with.

"Thank you," Mr Cutty said, starting out of the flat again, making his way carefully around the broken glass.

On her way out, Julia gave the living room a cursory glance from the hallway. A ball of yarn sat on the sofa with a pair of knitting needles protruding from it. In fact, the flat's furniture was covered with knitted throws and blankets, which looked like they were probably home-made. Beatrice had done an admirable job of brightening up what would otherwise have been a rather utilitarian flat.

She paused at the little side table nestled by the sofa. There was a small pile of open post lying on top of it. Julia gave it a careful nudge with her fingernail so she could read the top few letters. They all seemed to be from various charities, thanking Beatrice for donations. None of them seemed to be huge amounts, but they must have added up if Beatrice was doing that regularly. If she had been embezzling money, it seemed she wasn't lavishing it on herself.

Julia hurried after Mr Cutty as he led the way down the stairs again. He spoke over his shoulder at her as she caught up. "I've got some contact details in the car I can give you," he said. "If you come by my office towards the end of the day tomorrow, say 5.30, we might have been able to find some more names by then. I've got my IT guy working overtime going over all Beatrice's work."

Chapter 2

Home was calling to Julia. Home, hearth and hound.

But there was somewhere they needed to stop on the way. If they were going to get their mitts on the 999 recording of the unfortunate Beatrice's last moments then their best chance was Mark's dad, Detective Inspector Rhys Jones.

The sun was well and truly set now, and the traffic had thinned out to a few sparse cars as Mark traversed the outskirts of King's Barrow.

Julia had the file Mr Cutty had given them open on her lap, although really it was just a few sheets of A4 in a cardboard sleeve.

Beatrice Campbell's face looked up at her. She had glossy brown hair, high cheekbones and thin lips. She would have been a very pretty young woman if her face wasn't pursed into a scowl. Julia stared down at the photo, flashing light and dark as they passed under the street lamps. Embezzler or not, Beatrice deserved to have her killer brought to justice, every bit as much as Mr Cutty deserved his freedom.

Julia flipped the file shut and began picking absent-mindedly at a fingernail as the houses rolled past outside. Something about the flat had been bothering her ever since they had left it and she gave a frustrated sigh.

"What's up?" Mark asked. "The Jeeves doorbell thingy," Julia said.

"What about it?"

"Didn't that seem a bit out of place? There was no smart TV in the flat. No smart speaker. She didn't even bother keeping her phone charged. She was only a little older than us and she had a landline."

Mark drummed his fingers thoughtfully on the steering wheel. "You're saying that she wasn't particularly attached to her gadgets," he said.

"Exactly," Julia replied.

"Well, strange or not, I think we need to see the photos that it took," Mark said.

The van bumped up over the curb and came to a halt on the broad sweep of the driveway outside Mark's family home, just in front of the bay windows where a line of warm yellow light was escaping through a gap in the curtains.

"Hopefully your dad can help us out with them," Julia said as she unbuckled and got out of the van.

"Yes, hopefully," Mark said, following her out and heading towards the house.

Mark reached out for the door handle but before he touched it the door flew open and there stood his dad, the detective inspector. He was still wearing his suit from work but the shirt was untucked and slightly ruffled-looking and he had a tumbler of something in one of his large hands.

Also, rather out of character for the inspector, beneath his bristly white moustache he was wearing a huge grin.

"Ah," Jones said, taking a step back so they could enter, "if it isn't Biddle Rhyne's two newest gumshoes."

Julia's heart sank as she stepped onto the plush red carpet inside and shed her coat. "You've heard then," she said.

"Yes, I've heard," Jones said. "I've hardly stopped laughing since Mark phoned me. What's the matter? Do you need to supplement the income from the bookshop?"

"I wasn't planning on charging," Julia said as she hung her coat on the peg.

A massive guffaw escaped Jones's lips. "Oh, that just makes it even funnier."

"And what exactly do you have against PIs, Dad?" Mark asked as he kicked his shoes off.

His dad got his laughter under control and held his hands out defensively. "I just think certain things need to be left to the professionals, that's all," he said.

Julia reflected grimly that if she'd left her case to the professionals then in all likelihood she would be sitting in a cell right now, wrongly convicted of murder. Since she needed Jones's help it didn't seem the right time to rake him over the coals for it, but a gentle nudge to remember the fact for himself might be useful.

"Even the professionals need a bit of help sometimes," she said softly.

Jones's grin only grew. "Look, the only time private investigators are ever helpful to anyone is if they have some useful idiot on the police force feeding them information."

Julia and Mark both lapsed into silence, and Mark leaned an elbow onto the top of the banister as they looked at him.

The grin slowly melted from Jones's face. "It's like that, is it? Well I'm not telling you anything."

"You're not going to do the 'useful' part, you mean?" Mark said.

Jones took a long sip of whatever it was he had in his glass. "Even if I did want to help you – and I don't – I can't. It's Freiland's case, not mine. I don't have any of the details."

Julia and Mark had been interviewed by DI Freiland when Julia had stumbled upon a murder outside the Barley Mow pub, where she'd been working at the time. At any rate, Freiland had seemed to be a very capable, no-nonsense sort of detective, although it was obvious there was no love lost between her and Jones. "She seemed very by the book," Julia said.

"Exactly," Jones replied. "By the book. So she's not going to go leaking details to a couple of newly minted gumshoes."

Julia looked despondently at Mark. That seemed to put paid to any chance of getting easy access to the case details from the police. By the long look on his face, Mark was thinking the same thing.

"Well, I suppose we should still talk to her, just in case," Mark said.

"Please do," his dad said enthusiastically. "And let me know when you do because that's a conversation I want to listen to."

"Oh, lay off, Dad," Mark said and stamped past him towards the living room.

"Wash your hands, dinner's almost ready," Jones called after him.

* * *

Julia shut the front door softly behind her and crept into her house, the sound of Mark's van fading away as it made its way up the road.

The front door opened straight into the living room, although the back of the sofa and armchair provided a half wall of sorts. The standard lamp was on in the corner, throwing a small amount of light over the living room, but it looked like it was unoccupied.

Julia felt completely drained after the long day and Jones's attitude all through dinner had done nothing to help matters. She had been hoping to quickly greet her pet terrier – something which always improved her mood – and sneak to bed without running into her housemate and facing yet more ridicule.

Fate, it seemed, was not on her side though. Rumpkin remained snoring loudly on his rug under the stairs and, just as Julia had kicked her shoes off and was preparing to tiptoe away, the kitchen door opened. A voluminous pink dressing gown emerged through it, containing Sally within. A mug of something steamed in her delicate hands, possibly dreamtime tea by the smell of it.

"You're home late," Sally said. "I had assumed you were at Mark's, or I'd have made you one."

"I was at Mark's," Julia said. "But I just needed to talk to his dad."

"Oh?"

"There was a man in the shop asking for help with something," Julia said.

Sally's features creased into a frown. "Help from Rhys?"

Julia's shoulders slumped. The last thing she needed tonight was to be made fun of again, but she might as well get it over with. She explained about how Ronald Cutty had come into the bookshop asking for help clearing his name, and what had followed.

"You're not going to laugh, are you?" Julia asked as she concluded.

"Laugh? Why would I laugh? What's remotely funny about it?" Sally said.

"Rhys thought it was funny," Julia said with a sigh. "Me and Mark investigating the murder, I mean."

"Well Rhys is an oaf," Sally said, a statement which Julia was inclined to agree with. "And there's more than one person behind bars thanks to you already, so he should think about that before he laughs."

Julia allowed herself a slight smile. "Thanks, Sally," she said. "But he's probably right. If he won't help, or his colleague Freiland, then what hope do I really have? I might as well tell Ronald he needs to find someone else."

Sally clicked her tongue thoughtfully. "You said that you already had the name of one of the embezzlement victims? They're a suspect, right?"

"I have a name," Julia said. "Mr Peabody, at the council."

Both she and Mark had raised their eyebrows when they'd seen his name in the file which Mr Cutty had given them. They'd crossed paths with Mr Peabody before in his role as the planning inspector when they were doing the bookshop conversion. Evidently working in the local council meant wearing a lot of different hats as it appeared Mr Peabody was the parish clerk too.

"Oh," said Sally, looking a little deflated. "He didn't really come across as the violent type, did he?"

"No," Julia agreed. "And besides, would he care enough about the council's money going missing that he would go out and hurt someone? It wasn't like it was his own money."

"True," Sally said. "Then again he did seem to take his responsibilities at the council rather seriously."

Julia hummed. That was true but she was still unconvinced. "I guess it's somewhere to start."

Sally beamed. "Exactly!"

* * *

Julia walked briskly along Biddle's high street, which was straight and narrow. Despite the constant rush of cars streaming towards King's Barrow, the pavements were largely clear and only a few times did Julia have to squeeze in against the buildings to let people pass.

The cold weather was beginning to ease now. A few of the window boxes even had colourful little flowers in them, doing their best to struggle open and liven up the street with what little sunlight they got this early in the spring.

She turned off after the hairdresser's, which used to be the post office, and the older buildings of the high street gave way to more recently built family homes. Some of them still had little frontages of grass but most had sprouted blockwork in front of them, on which the family cars were parked.

The houses were all different shapes and sizes, although mostly from the same 1970s era with the occasional more recent interloper. But they all had one thing in common: they were all very tidy. The lawns, where they existed, were mown short despite the rapid growth of the grass at this time of year. The windows were clean. The cars all shone. It was clear that the people who lived in these houses took pride in their homes.

On the whole, Julia liked Biddle Rhyne. The people were generally friendly and when they weren't, they tended to at least not be friendly in interesting ways. She had lived here over half her life now and couldn't imagine living anywhere else.

She was on her way to the council offices. Mark had agreed to open the shop that morning. He'd been surprisingly keen to accept the duty, in fact. Julia had been grateful, but as she'd set off she realized he was avoiding going to work and getting on with the painting. She wasn't sure what it was about his latest job that he disliked so much. He'd never been workshy; they'd never have gotten the bookshop open at all if it hadn't been for his fairly tireless efforts to renovate it. But he seemed to be dodging his current site at every opportunity.

Julia had reached the gates of the rather bland, single-storey building which housed the parish council and its denizens. Whatever was on Mark's mind, she'd have to figure it out later on. Right now she needed to concentrate on the task at hand.

The twin doors slid back automatically as Julia approached and she stepped into the open, airy space of the entry foyer. The black swivel seat behind the reception desk was vacant, so she scanned the board of offices next to it before carrying on down the hallway.

Julia knocked on the flimsy wooden door that bore Mr Peabody's name. She wasn't relishing another encounter with him. It would be unfair to say that the man was unfriendly. It was more that he didn't seem to understand the concept of what a friend was, or why someone would want them. If you could have distilled the town planning regulations and put them into human form, then you would have someone very much like Mr Peabody.

A voice inside called for her to come in so she opened the door and stepped through.

"Good morning," said the man seated behind the desk.

Julia blinked. "Oh, I'm sorry. I was looking for Mr Peabody."

"That is I," the man said, straightening his tie. He certainly had the same fastidious dress sense, but he was slightly pudgy with thinning sandy hair on top of his head and pale-blue eyes.

"Perhaps you were looking for my husband, the other Mr Peabody?" the man suggested.

Julia smiled. That would explain it. "I think that's probably right," she said.

The Mr Peabody in front of her pointed at the door with the tip of a pencil. "You'll find the planning department down the hallway on the right," he said.

"No, it was you that I wanted to speak to," Julia said.

"But you just said the opposite."

"No, I was expecting the other Mr Peabody. But it's you that I wanted to talk to."

"But we're different people. You do understand that?"

"Yes, I do," Julia said. "But you're the parish treasurer, right?"

"That is correct."

"I'm glad that's settled," Julia said, and lowered herself into the thinly padded chair in front of the desk.

"If you're sure," Mr Peabody said.

"I'm here as a private investigator on the case of Beatrice Campbell," Julia said.

Mr Peabody sucked his lips together like he was trying to swallow a lemon. "What an absolutely horrible piece of business that was."

"Yes," Julia agreed.

"Tens of thousands of pounds gone, just like that," Mr Peabody said, his hands remaining quite immobile on the desk as he spoke. "I was just looking through our accounts at the end of the week as an amusing diversion from some of the more mundane treasury business and that's when I noticed the discrepancy."

"Perhaps you haven't heard," Julia said, treading carefully. "But I was referring to Miss Campbell's murder. She was found dead in her flat last week."

"Yes, I did hear about that," Mr Peabody replied.

Julia waited for a moment, expecting him to add 'how terrible' or 'I was so shocked to hear that' but he remained silent and bolt upright in his seat, so she continued.

"I was wondering if you'd mind accounting for your whereabouts on the night of her death," Julia said.

From her handbag, she produced a tiny notebook that she'd stolen from Jones and read out the date.

"Certainly." Mr Peabody cracked a smile. "Accounting is what I do. Excuse me, a little professional humour." He seemed to read Julia's expression because he added, "I should really leave the jokes to my husband, he's the funny one."

That gave Julia pause. If the other Mr Peabody was the one with the sense of humour then she shuddered to think what she was dealing with now on the other side of the desk.

Mr Peabody continued. "But, yes, I was working here until six. I signed out on the sheet. Then I caught the number 12 bus from the stop on the high street. That was around sixteen minutes later, the bus was eight minutes late."

Julia was scribbling frantically to get all of this down. She made a mental note to ask Jones about a shorthand system or something because frankly she wasn't keeping up.

"Then I did my shopping in King's Barrow and caught the bus back," said Mr Peabody. "Twelve minutes late that time. Then finally signed in about 9.30 p.m., although I'd have to check the records for an exact time."

Julia scrawled the last of this down and looked up. "Signed in where, sorry?"

"At home," Mr Peabody replied.

Julia noted that down. "Of course."

She looked back over her notes. Most of it was illegible, but she could remember the gist. He'd left work here, she could verify that, then done his shopping in King's Barrow and made his way back home.

"Is there anything else you need?" Mr Peabody asked.

"No, that's been very thorough. Thank you, Mr Peabody," she said.

"Not at all, it's been my pleasure to help. I look forward to seeing you if there's another crime you're investigating. Are you okay to see yourself out?"

Julia nodded as she rose from her chair and made her way back to the reception area.

Since she'd been in Mr Peabody's office, a woman had appeared with a short stepladder and was stringing red, white and blue bunting across the wall, over the top of a noticeboard. She was humming softly to herself while she worked.

Judging that the coast was clear, Julia stepped quietly over to the still vacant reception desk and scanned the raised public-facing partition. There was a stack of flyers in front of her and next to it an out-of-hours sign-in book with a mangled-looking biro lying beside it.

With a quick look over her shoulder, Julia flipped the sign-in book open and ran her eyes down the list of names on the most recent page.

She had to suppress a chuckle. The only name on the list was 'Mr Peabody' repeated over and over again. She would put good money on it that it was his own system and he was the only one to use it.

Actually, no, Julia corrected herself. 'Mr Peabody' appeared in two different handwritings. It seemed both men used the system. At any rate there was an entry for Mr Peabody on the date of Beatrice's death, after the time of the 999 call.

Not that that proved much. Julia made a mental note to check out his alibi at the supermarket when she got the chance. But deep down she was pretty certain this wasn't her man.

"Oh, hello there. Can I help you?" A cheery voice came from behind her.

Julia flipped the book shut as stealthily as she could, keen to avoid being stigmatized in the village as a snoop, no matter how true that might be.

She grabbed hold of one of the flyers as she turned around.

"I was just having a nose of this," Julia said to the woman who was slowly and unsteadily lowering herself from the stepladder.

Julia glanced at the flyer she was holding.

The village fête was coming up. She should have known from the bunting, it was a big deal in the village every spring.

The village fête had good pedigree, going back to the 1930s. Apparently on one occasion during the war a Hurricane had been downed just outside Biddle Rhyne while the fête was going on and the locals had all rushed to save the pilot.

There was usually some sort of parade to mark the event. If it didn't rain too heavily. The rescue was a point of pride for some in Biddle Rhyne, although from how Julia had heard it told, the rescue party had streamed out of one of the local pubs. The village fête seemed to have been a bit more of a prospect in the past. Her memories of attending the fête when she was younger were pleasant enough, but it was always a little dull. This year would surely be the same.

Something else on the flyer caught Julia's eye.

"A bake-off," she murmured.

The woman's face lit up as she folded the ladder up and came tottering over. "Oh, yes," she said. "Do you fancy entering?"

"Maybe," Julia said thoughtfully. She'd taken up baking recently, and secretly felt she'd made rapid progress. Although she would definitely need to practise if she was going to keep up with Sally.

"The competition might be fierce," the woman warned her. "We'll see if anyone can unseat Mrs Burns. She took first place last time we had one."

Julia remembered, dimly. Allegations of cheating had abounded. The whole thing had gotten quite heated. In hindsight that was probably why the bake-off hadn't featured for a few years.

Still, she only had to enter for fun. It might prove relaxing.

Julia pushed the flyer into her handbag and smiled.

"I'll think about signing up," she said.

Chapter 3

The bell jangled overhead as Julia stepped from the small entry foyer and onto the shop floor, one of the peculiarities of working in a shop converted from the village library.

From the stool behind the planed wooden counter, Mark straightened up and smiled. He was dressed in jeans and a crisply ironed black shirt. It was the smartest that Julia had seen him dressed in a while. Evidently he took his role as shop assistant seriously.

Bookshelves rose up in two tall rows, leaving only a narrow strip of carpeted floor to walk down. The ancient, towering, intricately carved shelves were made of dark wood. Part gift and part apology from her old boss after the previous set of shelves were reduced to kindling by one of his contractors. Already it seemed the young shop had quite a bit of history to it.

As striking as the shelves were, they did block off most of the light that came in from the windows overlooking the high street. Julia hoped that the effect was 'snug' rather than 'gloomy'. But that was for the customers to determine. When they had any.

Julia brushed down the nearest line of shelves and leaned over the counter to greet Mark with a peck on the cheek. "Thanks again for watching the shop," she said.

She studied his reaction closely, but he seemed perfectly happy, displaying a cheery smile, and a twinkle in his eyes from the overhead lights. "Not at all," he said. "How did it go with Mr Peabody?"

"Well…" Julia hopped up to perch on the counter next to the till and filled Mark in on what had transpired at the council offices.

"He doesn't sound like a ruthless killer," Mark said when she finished.

"I'm fairly sure he'd feel duty-bound to turn himself in to the police if he so much as accidentally broke the speed limit," Julia said.

Mark shuffled on the stool. "Maybe Mr Cutty will have more promising leads when we see him this afternoon."

"Well let's hope so, for his sake," Julia said.

"And I still think we should talk to DI Freiland," said Mark.

"Despite what your dad says?"

"All the more reason. I've never listened to him," Mark replied.

"And look where it got you," Julia said. "Dating a bookshop owner who bleeds you dry and doesn't even mind her own store."

"Well, business has been booming while you were away," Mark said.

"Really?" Julia asked.

"Yes," said Mark. "Someone came in asking for directions and I flogged them a local history book."

"Which one?"

"I don't know, does it matter? I also sold one of the baking books," said Mark proudly.

"There might be a bit of a rush on those," Julia said. "Look." She dug through her handbag until she found the flyer and smoothed it out on the countertop.

Mark's eyes lit up. Julia fancied she could hear him salivating. "Oh, a bake-off," he exclaimed. "You should get Sally to enter."

Julia snatched the flyer up again, scrunching it in the process, and stuffed it back into her bag. "I thought I might enter," she said, pointing her nose into the air.

"That would be good too," Mark mumbled.

Julia slid from the counter back to the floor and stalked round behind the till. "Anyway I'm back now, I can take over here."

Mark looked, if anything, even more dejected as he shifted from the stool.

Julia relented. "How is work at the site going?" she asked him as he shrugged into his jacket.

"Oh, fine, fine," he said glumly. "Work's work, isn't it? Painting one wall is a lot like painting another. I'll pick you up at five and we can head to Cutty's and co."

Julia frowned. Mark was usually so enthusiastic about his work and it wasn't like him to be like this, with shoulders slumped and head down.

The chime of the bells died away as he left the shop and Julia craned to look round the side of the shelves and watch him walk slowly past the window, hands in his pockets, to where his van was parked haphazardly on the pavement.

She sighed. Hopefully the shop would start bringing in some proper money soon. She didn't like the idea that he was taking naff jobs just to make up for the money he'd sunk into this place.

Julia padded over to the cookery section and selected a baking book at random, taking it back to the counter to pore over while she waited for a customer. Hopefully the fête would drive a few more sales in the baking section. She thought idly about putting a window display together as she flicked the pages of glossy photos of remarkable-looking cakes which she knew deep down she couldn't bake.

* * *

The accountancy firm Cutty and Partners turned out to be a tall, Georgian building of pale-yellow brick broken up by white sash windows. It was located on the nearside of King's Barrow, not very far from Beatrice's home, on a largely residential street which proved to be almost impossible to park on.

After Julia had dismissed Mark's initial suggestion of just bunging the hazards on and parking anyway, they had found a spot a few streets away and made their way back on foot.

Julia squinted at the back of Mark's neck and scratched some flecks of paint off.

"Hey," he said, swatting at her.

"We need to look presentable in front of clients," Julia said.

"Clients pay," Mark said, as he climbed the steps at the front of the building.

He pushed the decorative enamel doorbell with his finger and waited. Light was spilling out from beneath the door and they could hear the buzz of the bell deep inside the building. Listening carefully, Julia could hear someone banging about on the other side of the thick wooden door but no one answered.

Julia tried again, stretching past Mark to press the button. Again they could hear the bell on the other side of the wall and someone thumping about, but the door remained shut. The sun had set now and the evening began to chill as clouds rolled in overhead. Julia pulled her light coat tighter around her and wished she'd worn something a bit warmer.

Mark huffed and before Julia could stop him he pounded on the door with his fists, the deep banging echoing away inside.

A second later the door swung inwards and a man stood in its place, glaring out at them.

"What?" he demanded.

He was a tall man, and broad as well. He almost filled the generous doorframe of the building. He had a bald head – hard to tell if it was shaved or forced upon him by nature – more than compensated for by a tangle of bushy, black beard which blended into the dark hoodie he was wearing. Despite how baggy his clothing was, it was clear there was a decent amount of bulk to him.

His raised voice and his furious expression gave Julia pause before she answered, stuttering slightly. "We're here to see Mr Cutty," she said.

"And do I look like a receptionist?" the man said.

Before Julia could answer, a woman also appeared in the doorway, or what was left of it to appear in. She was almost as tall as the man but very slightly built. It looked like a decent gust of wind might send her sprawling. She was neatly dressed in office wear: a striped grey shirt and mid-length black skirt, with thick-looking tights and a cardigan over the top. She looked maybe a few years older than Julia, her blonde hair, pale enough to be almost white, swept back over the shoulders of her cardi.

She patted the man's considerable biceps in a conciliatory way, fingerless gloves covering her hands. "Come on, Dillon, that's enough," she said gently.

The man, Dillon apparently, remained unmoved, although Julia saw his expression softening.

"There's lots of work to do, I'm sure you don't have time for this," the woman said.

Dillon grunted and moved away, disappearing from view.

The woman gave an apologetic smile and pivoted sideways to allow them access.

Julia stepped up through the doorway, finding herself in a brightly lit corridor with corporate art on one wall and a line of doors on the other. Given the grand exterior of the building, the inside was surprisingly bland. She glanced in both directions down it, but Dillon was nowhere to be seen.

Mark followed her in. "What's the deal with him? Was he cheaper than a pit bull?"

The woman sighed. "You'll have to excuse Dillon, he's been under a lot of pressure recently. I assume that you're Ford and Jones, the detectives?"

"That's us," Mark said smartly, extending a hand. "Mark Jones."

Doing her best to smile, Julia shook hands afterwards; the woman's fingers, or at any rate what emerged from the glove, were icy cold.

"I'm Ginny Stroup," the woman said. "Ronald is expecting you, but I'm afraid he's on a call right now. Things have been a bit manic here ever since Beatrice's extracurriculars came to light. Dillon's our IT manager. He's been working overtime trying to trace where everything's gone and provide the police access to all of Beatrice's logins."

"He works in IT?" Mark said, raising an eyebrow.

Ginny nodded as she shut the door on the gathering dusk outside. "That's right. He's generally very good, when he's not doing his Incredible Hulk impression. Like I said it's been a tough time, you'll have to excuse him. And to be fair, he shouldn't have needed to stop to answer the door, we have an intern for that sort of thing, wherever he's got to."

As she finished speaking, annoyance evident in her tone, Ginny reached out to one of the internal doors and threw it open.

The light spilling through from the corridor revealed an empty room, although it was a stretch even to call it that; it was barely more than an alcove. The narrow space had a desk – unoccupied – shoved against one wall, but that was about it in the way of furnishings. On the other side of the desk was another door, a fire exit by the looks of it.

Ginny tutted as she pulled the door closed again. "Looks like Gary's knocked off early again. I've warned him about that."

She gave a belaboured sigh. "Let me take you on to Mr Cutty's office and we'll see if he's available."

Julia and Mark followed her as she led the way down the corridor. Each of the doors they passed had a name plaque set beneath a frosted glass panel. Julia noticed Ginny's name on one of the plaques. Other than her office, the lights all seemed to be off inside the rooms. In spite of what she had said about the intern, it seemed that most of the firm weren't inclined to work late.

"You'll have to excuse the cold," Ginny said, lowering her voice slightly. "Mr Cutty is such a cheapskate when it comes to the heating. In winter you could see your breath in here. Can you imagine? I know people call us accountants 'bean counters', but really, can you imagine?"

Julia tutted. She had plenty of experience with cheapskate bosses. At least work at the pub had tended to be warm though. It didn't matter if the log fire was for the customers' sake, it warmed the staff as well.

"Is he a difficult man to work for then?" Mark asked.

Ginny glanced back over her shoulder as she walked. "Oh, no, I wouldn't say that. Other than the heating thing he's been a wonderful boss, really. Generous Christmas bonus. He pushed to get the paid maternity leave extended. And he gives that lump of an intern umpteen second chances." Her tone became rather dry as she finished speaking.

Reaching the end of the corridor, Ginny leaned forward and put her ear to the final door.

"It sounds like he's still on a call in there," she said quietly as she straightened back up. "I'm sure he won't be long."

Despite all of her smiles, Ginny had deep lines underneath her eyes. Understandable given the circumstances, Julia supposed. She picked unconsciously at her nails as they stood waiting.

"Is that a hint of an accent I heard?" Mark asked her.

Ginny nodded. "You have a good ear. Yes, I lived in California until I was fourteen. That's longer ago now than I care to admit, but it still slips through from time to time. Ah, I think I heard him finishing up."

Ginny knocked gently on the door and stuck her head round. "Go on in," she said to them.

Julia thanked her and stepped into Mr Cutty's office. Mark followed her in and Ginny hovered in the doorway.

The place was chaotic. Two different laptops were open on the desk and paper was strewn about in stacks and individual sheets, with little order to them as far as Julia could discern.

There were two chairs in front of the desk, but since they too were stacked up with paper, Julia and Mark remained standing.

Mr Cutty leaned forward in his high-backed office chair as they entered. His tie was askew and his top button undone. What hair he had left was similarly disarrayed. He did his best attempt to smile as they came in. "Thanks for coming." He pushed an open tin of biscuits towards them across his crowded desk, dislodging a folder onto the floor in the process, although he didn't appear to notice. "Do help yourself," he said.

Julia gave a quick glance down at the tin. It was empty save for a few crumbs and a sorry-looking chocolate chip which looked like it had melted at some point earlier in the day. "Thanks," she said. "I'm fine."

"Did you pay Mr Peabody a visit?" Mr Cutty asked. "Was it fruitful?"

"Not a huge amount," Julia said. "We still need to verify his alibi but it looks fairly tight."

Mr Cutty chewed on the top of his pen. "Well, Dillon's managed to uncover another victim of Beatrice's activities," he said, his voice strained. "Maybe you'll have more luck there."

Julia slipped her notebook from her handbag and held her pen ready. "Who have you found?"

"His name's Finn Tinkler, he runs a small construction contractor," Mr Cutty said. He searched briefly through the papers in front of him before handing one to Julia. "His details are on there. Been one of our clients for years now. He was not a happy bunny when I told him."

Mr Cutty's eyes darted up to where Ginny was still standing in the doorway. "You don't fancy renewing your acquaintance with him, do you? I seem to remember he was fond of you, maybe you could mollify him a bit?"

Ginny snorted. "No thank you," she said, and disappeared back into the corridor.

"Ginny used to work that account," Mr Cutty explained, "but she asked to come off given that he was such a difficult man to work with, so we replaced her with Beatrice. Beatrice was such a pleasant woman, she got on with anyone."

"Funny then," Mark said, "maybe if Mr Tinkler had been a bit more pleasant then he might still have his money."

Julia glared daggers at him and quickly changed the subject. "As we were coming in, Ginny mentioned that you haven't been able to trace where the missing money has gone," she said.

Mr Cutty waved a hand at the piles of work on his desk. "No, we're still trying to disentangle it all. There was quite a web," he said. "Well, hopefully Dillon will have more for you soon. Both the names of the victims-slash-suspects and also a better idea of where the money's gone."

Mr Cutty turned his attention back to one of the laptops and began typing, so that seemed to be their cue to leave.

After exchanging a glance, Mark and Julia turned to go but Julia paused at the doorway. "Actually, there's one other thing that may help us," she said.

"I'm all ears," Mr Cutty said, finishing whatever he was typing and looking up over his screen. His face was washed blue in the glow of the monitor.

"The JeevesDoor camera," Julia said, making an effort not to add 'thingumajig' on the end.

"What about it?" said Mr Cutty.

"It seemed a bit of an odd thing for Beatrice to have. She didn't have anything else like that in her house that I could see. Gadget wise, I mean."

"Oh, right. I do know about that actually, because when she got it, she brought it into the office and got Dillon to help her set it up. I think her nephew bought it for her as a gift."

"You don't know the nephew's name, do you?" Mark asked.

Mr Cutty shook his head. "Sorry."

"We were also wondering if you had CCTV here," Julia said.

"Here?" said Mr Cutty, looking puzzled.

"If one of the embezzlement victims was looking for revenge on Beatrice, it's possible they followed her home. They'd already have known where she worked, but they might not have known her home address," Julia said.

Mr Cutty grimaced. "That's a nasty thought," he said.

Julia was inclined to agree. Something similar had happened a few months ago when one of her colleagues had met his premature end.

"We have a few cameras," Mr Cutty continued. "I've got access to the footage, although I'd have to remind myself how to view it. I can send it over to you later if you think it would be helpful."

"It might be. It will be worth looking at anyway," Julia said. "I think that's everything." She looked over at Mark and he gave a nod.

"Good night, Mr Cutty," Julia said.

"Ronald," he replied. "Good night."

"Sorry, Ronald," Julia corrected herself before following Mark out of the room. She closed the door behind them and they began to drift back down the corridor towards the exit.

"What was that remark about how Mr Tinkler should have been nicer?" Julia said in a harsh whisper. "That wasn't very professional."

Mark looked down and scuffed his foot as he walked. "Hm, sorry. I know the man. Ronald was right about him not being a very pleasant customer – the man's a real piece of work."

"How do you know him?" Julia asked.

"Oh, I've worked some jobs with him before. Or his company, rather; he hasn't had skin in the game himself for years now. I can tell you about it another time."

"Fine."

They trudged on down the corridor. There was only one other room with a light on now; right at the far end, the frosted glass panel was illuminated.

"Dillon's lair, I suppose," Mark said, nodding at it. "Do you think we should ask him about that doorbell camera if he set the thing up?"

Julia shook her head. "Not now at any rate. The mood he's in, I don't think we're going to get much out of him."

"Fair enough," Mark said, opening the door and stepping out onto the street.

Ginny hadn't been wrong, it was a draughty old building they were working from; it was warmer as they stepped out into the evening air, a few of the brighter stars managing to shine through overhead.

"I'll drive you home then?" Mark asked, as they walked down the empty pavement, the sound of traffic from the main road drifting over.

"Yes, I'm shattered," Julia said. "First thing tomorrow we can see if we can sweet talk Freiland. Your dad said she was a morning person."

"That only goes to show we're dealing with someone wholly unreasonable," Mark said. He looked past Julia at the abandoned street. "I still reckon we'd have been fine parking here."

Chapter 4

Julia rummaged in her handbag for her house keys. She and Mark had stopped in King's Barrow for food before he dropped her home. It was late now, and a quiet calm had settled upon the village.

Julia checked her phone as she continued to hunt for her keys. It was 8.30 p.m.

Finally she gained access to the house and stepped in. A pair of eyes watched her from around the back of the armchair, glinting in the dim light coming from the standard lamp in the corner.

"Hello boy," Julia said cheerfully.

There was a subdued woof and the eyes allowed themselves to close again and canine snoring floated across the living room.

Julia sighed as she tossed her coat onto the pile under the stairs and removed her shoes. "Yes, I missed you too, Rumpkin," she said, apparently to herself.

There was industrious noise coming from the kitchen and, as she got closer, inviting smells too. Baking was a major benefit of living with Sally. It had seen them through some rough patches. Julia turned the handle and pulled the door open.

Sally was in the kitchen, dressed in a luminous pink apron. Stacked around her on every available surface there were cakes. Cakes on cooling racks, cakes on the hob, cakes on the counters and cakes lined like soldiers on the shelf that held the recipe books. Some were steaming, smelling like they were fresh out of the oven, while others looked like they might be previous batches.

Those cakes that had been sliced revealed a chequered inside like a Battenberg, although the colours were vivid red and blue, with white icing quartering them.

Julia looked at them in wonderment. While she was used to Sally baking, the sheer scale of this was something altogether new. With a shaky hand Julia held out the crumpled flyer she'd picked up at the council offices.

"They're going to do a bake-off at the fête," she stammered.

Sally blew a stray blonde curl out of her face and plucked the flyer from Julia's hand before sending it arching towards the bin.

"Seen it," Sally said. "Seen it. Entered it. Going to win it."

Julia made a slow pivot, soaking in the bakery that had recently been her kitchen. "Yes I imagine you are," she said. "Do you really need this many cakes?"

"Practice makes perfect," Sally said, opening the oven door and pulling a tray out with a clatter.

Despite the non-negligible quantity of greasy food already congealing in her stomach, Julia reached out for the nearest slice of cake.

"Oi," Sally said sharply. "Hands off my Britainberg."

Julia glared. "Oh come on," she said. "You don't even have any space to put that one down."

Sally looked about her for a free surface. "Fine. But only one, and then you can clear some space for me."

Before she could change her mind, Julia plucked a square of the brightly coloured cake from the counter and popped it into her mouth. It was one of the best things she had ever tasted, although she wasn't about to give her friend the satisfaction of telling her that. "Mm, that's not bad," she managed.

"You're a poor liar, now make some room for this tray before it burns through my gloves," Sally said.

Julia obliged and began stacking some of the cooled slices on top of one another. "Let me have another, you can't possibly need all of these," Julia said.

Sally placed the tray down on the heatproof mat Julia had cleared. "They all have to go through quality control," she said.

"What quality control?" Julia asked.

A voice from the doorway made her jump. "This quality control."

Julia turned to see Charlie making his way into the kitchen. He'd only been dating Sally a couple of months, but Julia was pretty sure she was already noticing some extra pounds creeping on.

"You're not going to eat all of these," Julia said.

"I've been underestimated before," Charlie replied earnestly.

Julia rolled her eyes. "When you throw up, try and do it quietly, I need to concentrate," she said. "Now, if you'll excuse me, I have some investigating to do."

"Oh, yes, I heard about your new side business," Charlie said. "Next time you're cornered by a knife-wielding killer, please don't involve me in it."

"You involved yourself in that," Julia muttered and swept from the kitchen.

In the living room, she picked her laptop up from where it was lying atop a pile of books, cruelly deposited Rumpkin out of the armchair, and flipped the lid open.

Searching a combination of Beatrice Campbell's name and 'King's Barrow' turned up a dozen or so results in the local news. Skimming over them, Julia recalled reading one or two of them when they came out.

There was that pretty but perma-scowling face in each article. Julia had wondered if it was just an unflattering staff photo that Ronald had sent her. She could remember her own ID tag at the library, when it had still existed, hadn't exactly captured her good side. But despite Ronald saying how pleasant Beatrice had been with all the clients, it seemed that it had been her lot in life to go through the world always looking ticked off.

Scanning over the news articles, there were no immediate next of kin mentioned: no sons or daughters. But Julia had expected that, she knew Beatrice had lived alone and never started a family. Julia shook her head. She would never have the chance to now.

She did eventually find Beatrice's brother on Facebook, an older man living in Ireland, and from his page Julia found Beatrice's nephew.

"Tony Campbell," she muttered to herself.

He didn't seem to exist on Facebook, but after a bit of digging she did find an Instagram account.

Julia clicked to message him and hovered with her fingers over the keys. Blank introductions online were difficult at the best of times. Trying to introduce herself as a PI investigating his aunt's killer was trickier still.

Julia moistened her lips and started to type.

Hello Tony. You don't know me but I'm an investigator working on your aunt's case.

Julia paused to think. It was probably best to keep it a little vague and draw him in. Ultimately she wanted him to send her the photos that the doorbell had captured and he was probably unlikely to do that if he thought Julia was trying to get the only suspect in the case off the hook.

I had a few questions I was hoping you might be able to answer.

Julia sat and reread the message several times over before eventually conceding to herself that she wasn't going to think up anything more engaging than that and hitting send.

She waited a good while with one eye on the laptop screen to see if there was a response. Julia put the TV on and then off again, as there was never anything good on it. *The Green Knight* came off the bookshelf, one of those pilfered from Biddle Rhyne library before it was closed down for good. But it failed to hold Julia's attention.

She even risked going back into the kitchen to make tea. Sally and Charlie were washing up after the baking frenzy and fighting one another with the soap suds and giggling.

It was so awful Julia didn't even let her tea brew properly before retreating back to the safety of the living room.

Rumpkin was asleep on the floor by the armchair and snoring. Julia prodded him with her toe, first to try and quieten him and then just for fun.

Eventually, as the last of her barely palatable tea was just being drained from the mug, the laptop chimed and Julia uncoiled to pick it up, startling Rumpkin and sending him on a quiet barking spree.

"Hush," she chided him, looking eagerly at the laptop.

As it turned out, it wasn't Tony messaging her back. It was Ronald emailing through the CCTV footage from the day Beatrice had died.

I hope it's useful. The police called again after you left. They seem more convinced than ever that it was me.

Julia couldn't think of much to say by way of reply so she just clicked on the file and waited impatiently as it downloaded to her laptop, tapping her foot on the carpet.

* * *

The next morning the wind had picked up and rain was lashing down against the window when Mark let himself in. He had the collar of his polo shirt flipped up but it had provided little protection against the weather and just from walking the length of Julia and Sally's driveway he was looking wet and bedraggled.

But as Julia rose from the armchair to greet him, stepping over the dog snoring on the carpet, she could tell it wasn't just the rain making Mark look miserable.

"How was work?" she asked. They had planned to drive up to talk to DI Freiland and Mark had put in some early hours to make time.

Mark only answered her with a heavy shrug, but Julia really didn't need to be a detective to know something on this job was bothering him. Sooner or later she would have to find out what.

Mark gave her a brief, damp hug to say hello and nodded at the open laptop now perched on the coffee table. "How's the investigation going?" he said.

Julia led him round the side of the sofa into the living room. "Ronald sent the CCTV footage through last night," she said.

"Anything interesting?"

"Not that I could spot," Julia said. "But you can judge for yourself. I might have missed something."

As Mark settled onto the sofa cushions, Julia leaned forward and tapped the keys to show him what they had got.

"Here's Beatrice leaving. There's no timestamp but it's still light, so it seems she left before everyone else, like Ronald said she did."

Mark squinted at the screen. There were two camera angles. The first was inside the accountancy building, above their front door, and had captured Beatrice's face. The quality in the video, which was really just a series of still images, wasn't perfect. But the grainy resolution was enough to see it was clearly Beatrice and that she was quite angry.

The second angle was outside, with the camera evidently mounted over the front door although Julia hadn't noticed it when they had been standing there waiting to be let in. The resolution was even lower on this one, and the picture a wider angle. In a series of jerky stills it showed Beatrice as she stormed off away from the building.

"I can't see anyone follow her," Mark said, squinting at the pixels.

"No," Julia agreed. "Not even any cars on the street."

"What else do we have?" Mark asked.

Julia rolled the video on. "Nothing for a long time," she said. "Then we have the other employees leaving."

She slowed the video down for Mark to see. Ginny was first to leave and Dillon shortly after. Then there were a couple of employees she hadn't met. The firm's website had staff photos for everyone working there, except the recent intern who just had a generic silhouette of a person instead. Using that directory, Julia had managed to check that everyone on the video was an employee.

"And then Ronald leaves," Julia continued. "Again I can't see anyone following him."

Mark flung himself back into the sofa looking defeated and stared up at the ceiling. "Not a lot of use, was it?" he muttered.

Julia lowered the lid on the laptop with a click. "I guess not," she said. "Maybe the photos from the doorbell camera at Beatrice's will be more useful."

"If we can get hold of them," said Mark. It wasn't like him to be so defeatist.

Julia nestled up to him on the sofa. "You'll have to charm DI Freiland," she said. So far Beatrice's nephew hadn't replied to her message.

"Charming?" Mark said. "Me?"

"Yes, it's been known," Julia said.

Mark gave a sniff. "Have you been baking, Julia?" he asked. "It smells delicious."

"It's not mine, it's Sally's," Julia said. "And before you ask, you're not allowed any. She's being a real so-and-so about it, even though she's given Charlie enough to feed an army."

"Do we have any CCTV in the house?" Mark asked.

"Huh?" Julia said. "No."

Mark dislodged her and got up from the sofa. "Good, because I'm going in," he said, tiptoeing theatrically across the carpet.

Julia smiled and watched him go but he only got two steps before treading on the tip of Rumpkin's tail. The dog woke with a yowl.

She sighed. They were going to have to up their game if they were going to make it as detectives.

Chapter 5

The desk sergeant at King's Barrow Police Station was lounging on their chair behind the glass screen. Julia couldn't help but suspect he was surreptitiously reading a book underneath the counter.

His eyes flickered up as he heard her and Mark approaching and then with visible effort pulled himself more upright, smoothed down his uniform and gave them a brief smile in greeting.

"Here to see your dad, are you, Mark?" the sergeant asked.

"That's right," Mark replied.

The sergeant sent them through with a little wave of his hand.

Julia followed Mark as he made his way through the swinging doors into the main station and then into the large open-plan room where the detectives had their desks.

Jones's desk was empty, save for the jumble of manilla folders and the dock for his laptop. But then they'd already known that would be the case, they'd seen him leaving the station before they came in.

They made their way over to where Freiland sat, tapping smartly away at her keyboard at her desk on the other side of the room, next to the window.

"I did wonder if I'd be seeing you two," she said, still typing away.

"Yes, we wanted to talk to you about Ronald Cutty's case," Julia said.

"I'm sure you do," Freiland replied without looking up.

Julia sighed. She wasn't going to get the detective's full attention. She might as well just launch into it.

"The evidence against him is circumstantial at best," Julia said, wondering if she'd used the word correctly. "Anyone could have come in through Miss Campbell's window, locking it behind them and leaving through the front door."

"Anyone capable of scaling twelve feet of vertical wall and then slipping in through a narrow window which the victim, through happenstance, left open during a cold snap, you mean?" Freiland finally removed her hands from the keyboard and looked up at Julia.

The detective continued. "Furthermore they must have done this all within the narrow window of time after Mr Cutty was caught on camera at the victim's flat and before Miss Campbell dialled 999. A call in which Miss Campbell used her final breaths to name Mr Cutty, erroneously, as her killer?"

Julia swallowed. Freiland certainly made the case seem more damning than Ronald Cutty had done himself. But she'd seen the look in his eye when he asked for help, and she recognized a bit of her own past reflected back at her. At least, she thought she did. She pressed on.

"Actually, that doorbell camera you mentioned. We were hoping that it might have caught something useful."

"It did catch something useful," DI Freiland replied. "It caught Mr Cutty entering the flat."

"No, I meant," Julia stammered, "I mean, would it be possible to have a look at the photos?"

"Give two unqualified civilians calling themselves PIs access to evidence in a murder investigation? No, that's not possible," Freiland said.

Julia opened her mouth to plead their case again but Freiland carried on. "I've wasted enough time already. You two get out of here before I have you arrested as well."

"For what?" Mark said, eyes shining defiantly.

"For whatever I feel like," Freiland said. She knitted her fingers behind the back of her head and smiled. "You know, I've always wanted to say that."

Mark allowed himself a laugh. "Oh, you were joking."

"Not even a little," Freiland said. "Now beat it."

Julia and Mark looked at one another but there was nothing for it. The detective appeared to be serious and Julia didn't fancy spending any further time in police custody.

Tails between their legs, they made their way back out of the detectives' area into the corridor.

A familiar figure was lounging against the opposite wall, blowing gently on a coffee to cool it down.

"Go well, did it?" Jones said, a merry sing-song cadence enhanced by his usual Welsh lilt.

Julia didn't reply. Holding her head up as high as she could manage she strode back out to the reception area.

Proceeding at quite a clip through the swing doors, she almost collided with the huge mountain of flesh on the other side.

"Oh, I am sorry," Julia said, staggering back a step.

"No, no, my fault," a deep voice rumbled back at her.

She found herself looking up at Dillon, the IT specialist from the Cutty and Partners accountancy firm, clutching to his chest something in a clear plastic bag. He was still an intimidating figure, towering over Julia like he did, but he no longer had veins bulging in anger. In fact he had a look of contrition when he looked at her and Mark.

"Ah, I didn't realize the two of you were with the police, I should have realized," Dillon said. "I was having rather a bad day when you arrived, I'm sorry about that."

"That's quite all right," Julia said softly, deciding it best not to correct him.

Dillon extended his tree trunk arms, offering out the bag which Julia now saw contained two laptops, which looked chunky and rather old.

"I've managed to dig up two of Beatrice's previous devices. The last admin guy left me quite a mess, as I expect your colleagues told you. No records, no admin rights to let me log in. But I did manage to unlock them in the end," he said, smiling helpfully.

Julia kept her hands at her sides. "You can leave them with the desk sergeant," she said. Pilfering evidence was perhaps a step too far. "Was it very difficult?" she asked him.

"Was what difficult?" Dillon asked back.

"Gaining access to them, without the admin rights," said Julia.

"Oh." Dillon shrugged. "Not too difficult, I guess. All of Beatrice's old passwords were some combination of her birthday and her address. When I took over, I had to give her a bit of a chewing out because she used to just write them on Post-it notes and stick them next to her desk. IT

45

security wasn't her strong point apparently. I'll just leave them at the desk then."

"Actually, there was something else we wanted to ask you, while we have you," Julia said. "Ronald mentioned that you helped Beatrice set up the JeevesDoor for her."

Dillon pulled a face. "Actually, no. She asked me to and I told her I wouldn't help. That's the problem with being in IT, everyone thinks you're their personal on-call support. Her nephew bought it for her, I told her to get him to do it."

Julia nodded but her heart dropped. They were only getting those photos if Tony messaged her back. "Okay, thanks," she said.

The door behind her swung open and she caught a glimpse of Freiland coming through.

Julia flashed a smile at Dillon. "Thanks again for your help, have a nice day."

With that she gave Mark a nudge and they hurried out of the building.

* * *

A high wall of red brick separated Finn Tinkler's property from the road, one of the many lanes that crossed the strip of countryside between King's Barrow and Biddle Rhyne.

Julia pressed the talk button on the metal intercom next to the gate and waited as rain pattered down on the top of the umbrella which Mark held aloft covering both of them.

Eventually there was a click and a muted voice spoke to them from the intercom. "Yes? Who is it?"

"Is that Mr Tinkler?" Julia asked.

"Yes, what do you want?"

"Hi. My name's Julia Ford. I'm an investigator looking into the accounts regarding Miss Beatrice Campbell. I believe you've already been in contact with my employer, Mr Cutty, of Cutty and Partners. I'm here to talk to you about the case."

Julia waited for Mr Tinkler to respond. Technically everything she had said was true, although she had been careful not to tell him that she was really there to ascertain if he had strangled Beatrice.

There was a long pause and then finally, without any further reply, the gates swung smoothly inward.

"Here, take the brolly," Mark said, holding the handle of the large green and white striped golf umbrella out towards her.

"Are you sure you're not coming too?" Julia asked him as she took it.

Mark shook his head. "I'll only antagonize him. Plus it will raise questions about us if he recognizes me from the worksite, although I'm not sure he's ever given me enough attention to notice. I'll wait in the van."

Julia said goodbye and hurried through the gates before they decided to close again.

It certainly looked like Mr Tinkler had done well for himself. A large, black luxury car sat on the driveway that led up to the house. On either side was a wide strip of garden, well-tended in the way that suggested it could only be someone's job to keep it so.

As Julia approached the double front door, with neoclassical pillars standing guard on either side, she half expected a uniformed butler to open them.

But it was Mr Tinkler himself. He was a short, stocky man, only a bit taller than Julia but much wider. His hair was already thinned out on top and despite being dressed neatly in a polo shirt and khakis, he had at least a day's worth of stubble.

"Any luck finding my money then?" he asked as he shut the door behind Julia.

Before waiting for a reply he began making his way off down the brightly lit corridor. He moved with an odd, stiff gait to his walk.

Julia shook the worst of the rain from her umbrella, put it into the stand by the door, and hurried after him. "We're working on it," she said. "I'm really here about Miss Campbell."

Mr Tinkler pushed open a door revealing an expansive study. The walls were bare, but there was a sizable glass desk placed in the centre of the carpet and Mr Tinkler, again moving stiffly, settled himself down into the office chair behind it. There were no other chairs so Julia stood in front of the desk, holding her handbag awkwardly.

"What about her?" Mr Tinkler asked, screwing his face up in distaste.

"Are you aware that Miss Campbell was strangled in her home last week?" Julia asked, watching him carefully for any subtle clues in his reaction.

She needn't have bothered. He cracked a grin and gave a short cackle of laughter. "Yeah, I heard about that. Couldn't have happened to a more deserving person, could it?"

He certainly seemed to have motive. He evidently liked his money and disliked anyone who separated him from it. "Are you aware there's an ongoing murder investigation?" Julia asked.

"Oh, I see," Mr Tinkler said. "You think I might have done it. Well, I can't say I blame whoever did it, it sounds like she had it coming. But, no, it wasn't me. Sadly her death will only make it harder to recover my money, won't it?"

"Anger can be a powerful motivator," Julia said, shifting uncomfortably on the spot.

"Sure, but do I look like I'm stupid, love?" Mr Tinkler asked. He tapped a few keys on the keyboard in front of him and then pivoted the monitor so Julia could see it.

She leaned in and found herself looking at Mr Tinkler's calendar.

"Anyway I was away on the day in question," Mr Tinkler said. "I was in Spain."

Julia nodded, looking at the calendar. It seemed that he was out of the country more often than he was in it. "You like to travel, I see, Mr Tinkler," she said.

He waved a hand over his shoulder at the rain sliding down the window pane. "It beats this miserable climate," he said.

Julia straightened up. Now that she thought about it, Mr Tinkler was rather tanned for the time of year. "Would you be able to send some travel documents to confirm your trip?" she asked.

"Not for you I won't, no," Mr Tinkler said. "For the police I will. Although from what I heard they've already got their man. Your boss, isn't it?"

Julia didn't reply. It wasn't public knowledge that Ronald was Freiland's prime suspect, and he hadn't been charged. Not yet, anyway. But she supposed that sort of news had a way of circulating.

Mr Tinkler rose. "Anyway, I have things to be getting on with. I only let you in because I thought you had something useful to say about my missing money. It seems you don't though, so, oh what's the expression I'm looking for? Get lost."

Mark must have seen her leave the house because he was waiting for her when she stepped outside the gates, braving the falling rain.

"Did you get anything useful?" he asked.

"Not really," Julia replied, handing the umbrella back so that Mark could hold it over them both. "And I see what you mean about him being unpleasant to work for. That's not a winning personality, is it?"

"It's not just his personality," Mark said. "He flogs his apprentices for every hour he can. Constantly finds ways to underpay. The whole site's miserable."

Julia ducked into the shelter of the van, the rain sounding louder once she was inside. Even if Mr Tinkler wasn't going to be forthcoming with details of his trip abroad, it would be odd to choose a lie that was so easy to verify.

Mark pulled away, and Julia got her phone out and found Mr Tinkler's social media. It seemed he hadn't been shy about sharing his holiday snaps with the world. There was a long set of photos showing him in the sun with various colourful drinks.

As she felt the chill rainwater seeping into the toes of her socks, she reflected that the world was not a particularly fair place.

Chapter 6

Julia was kneeling on the floor of the bookshop reshelving some of the books.

Earlier a couple of teenage girls had been in and spent a while picking through the shelves. It had got Julia's hopes up both at the prospect of a sale and at the quality of the youth of the day. But in the end the girls had left without a purchase, leaving books strewn behind them in their wake.

Julia slotted a hardback about horses back into its rightful place. She hadn't been that bad when she was their age, had she? Her mind drifted back to some of the things she and Sally had got up to when they were just a bit older than her so-called customers. Perhaps, on balance, a few temporarily de-homed books weren't the worst thing they could get up to.

The sound of the door opening made Julia peer round the edge of the bookshelf. She sighed, seeing Jones wandering in, and clambered upright.

"Hello, Rhys," she greeted him, wondering what he had in store for her today.

"Ah, Julia," he said, almost as though surprised to see her there in her own shop. "I think I owe you a bit of an apology. I might have gotten a bit carried away the other night. Some of the things I said might have been a little uncalled for, so I'm sorry."

Julia smiled. "Oh, that's okay, Rhys," she said. "No, I wasn't offended. That's fine."

The detective returned her smile, the corner of his moustache twitching, and he rubbed his hand up and down on the back of his neck distractedly. "And, erm, actually there was sort of something I wanted your help with," he said.

"Oh?"

"Yes." Jones stepped closer, lowering his voice. "There's a case I'm working on. Well it's proving a bit tricky and actually it's the sort of thing that maybe some outside help would be useful with. If you're not too busy that is."

"No, not at all," Julia said, although inwardly she wasn't sure where she would find any time between managing the shop and helping Ronald Cutty. "What is it?"

Jones reached around to his back pocket and pulled a folded sheet of paper out, handing it over to Julia.

She unfolded it.

"Missing Dog," she read.

She heard a sputtering sound and when she looked up, she was greeted with the sight of Jones turning beetroot red as he tried to contain his laughter.

"Yes. If you could keep your eyes peeled for Queen Beanie," Jones said.

"I will," Julia said stonily.

"Oh, and Julia?"

"Yes," she said.

Jones extended a finger and tapped the flyer. "£25 reward. It could be your first paying case!"

Julia screwed the flyer up into a ball inside her fist as Jones turned and saw himself out of the shop. She could hear him chuckling with laughter as he made his way through the foyer and out into the street.

She let the flyer fall into the waste-paper basket and did her best to calm down as she took up her seat by the till. Forcing herself to take measured breaths, she sat and waited for someone less oafish to grace the door. The time passed slowly and there were no customers, oafish or not. Julia checked her messages to see if Tony had replied, but he hadn't. Then she went to see if any of the shelves needed restocking, but they didn't.

Outside, the sun emerged from behind a cloud and illuminated the window display. It also illuminated an alarmingly large quantity of dust motes. She told herself, not for the first time, that she needed to use these quiet periods to dust. Actually, if she did that the place would be near spotless. She trailed back to the counter, knowing there was a duster behind there somewhere. But, before she could search for it, the bell above the door chimed and Julia craned forward to see who had come in.

It was Mrs Burns. She was a primly dressed woman of about sixty years old, with her hair pulled back in a tight bun and thin-framed glasses perched on the end of her nose.

She didn't bother to acknowledge Julia's smile before disappearing off between the shelves. She never did. Not that she was a regular customer, she acted the same way wherever she was. But she acted superior to everyone so Julia tried not to take it to heart.

While Mrs Burns browsed, Julia knelt down to look for the duster. She sifted through the stacks of paper. Invoices and bills mostly. They piled up along with the dust. At the back, possibly untouched since they'd first opened the doors, Julia spotted the duster and worked it free. It brought its own little cloud of dust with it as it came and Julia coughed, waving a hand in front of her.

Julia's head popped back over the top of the counter just in time to see Mrs Burns striding towards her. The older woman's gait was thrown off somewhat by the huge pile of books she was carrying.

Julia's eyes lit up at the sight of the potential sale. As Mrs Burns dropped the books onto the counter there was a satisfyingly solid thump. Julia suddenly found herself able to forgive a lot of Mrs Burns's transgressions.

"Ring them up, please," Mrs Burns said, which was about as close as she ever came to saying hello to Julia. Julia found that she could forgive this too.

Julia slipped the first book from the top of the stack and scanned the code. It was a baking book. Perhaps Mrs Burns was gearing up for the bake-off too. She was the reigning champion, wasn't she?

Julia rang up the second book. Also a baking book. She must be taking the competitions seriously.

Third book. Also baking.

Julia ran her eyes down the spines of the books. All of them baking. She looked up at Mrs Burns's face. Was there a hint of self-satisfaction on there? It was hard to tell.

"Just ring them up," Mrs Burns said.

Slower this time, Julia pulled the next book and added it to the total.

As she scanned the final book, it dawned on Julia what she was doing. She was trying to stymie the competition.

Since Mrs Burns rarely left Biddle Rhyne, or used a computer, perhaps it hadn't occurred to her that others might be able to get their books from a bit further afield.

It's an underhand tactic, Julia thought. But, a sale is a sale, and her spirits were lifted when she saw the total displayed on the till.

* * *

It was dark outside but the supermarket was, as always, evenly lit by the fluorescents overhead.

Julia was rather proud of her plan because she needed to get some shopping done anyway. King's Barrow was the closest place she was comfortable doing it, after the unfortunate incident she'd had at the village store in Biddle Rhyne. Once she had been an employee there, and after

Mrs White had been killed she had abandoned her post to go sleuthing. She hadn't explicitly been banned as a result, but the owner had given her such an earful that Julia had thought it wise not to set foot in there again.

It seemed that solving cases and working in a shop really didn't go well together. She should have learned from that before opening the bookshop, she thought to herself as the queue shuffled slowly along. Or at least before accepting Ronald Cutty's case.

In the wire basket held in the crook of Julia's arms was a large box of free-range eggs, butter, sugar and cocoa powder. She wasn't sure exactly what she was going to bake yet, but that covered most of the basics. She could improvise from there using whatever raw materials she could pilfer from Sally's supplies.

Julia would need to decide soon though. She needed to squeeze some proper practice in before the bake-off. And preferably before Sally wore the element out in the oven from overuse. The weekend was going to be busy.

Finally the man in front of Julia finished the elaborate bagging of his shopping and headed for the exit. As Julia stepped up to the till the young woman working there gave her an engaged smile. That was a good sign, she at least acknowledged the people she served, so perhaps she would remember if Mr Peabody had been there.

As the store worker picked up the flour and scanned it through, Julia unfolded a photo of Mr Peabody the treasurer which she'd printed off from the council website and showed it to her.

"Can I ask, do you remember this man being in here?" This was the time of day Mr Peabody claimed he did his shopping, so Julia hoped it might be the same checkout attendant who had served him.

The woman screwed her face up, the friendly smile falling away. Evidently she recognized him.

"Yes," she replied. "When he first came in he made a fuss about the 'Ten Items or Less' sign. Hard to forget him after that, as much as I'd like to."

"Oh, did he have an argument with someone over their basket?" Julia asked. Perhaps Mr Peabody had a hidden temper after all.

"No," the woman replied. "He just said that it should be 'Ten Items or Fewer' rather than 'Less'."

Julia nodded. "I see."

"He was quite insistent about it. He made me call the manager."

Julia suppressed a smile. It certainly sounded like she had the right person.

"Was he in here last Friday?" Julia asked.

The woman's eyes narrowed as she scanned the last of Julia's items and placed them next to the till. Julia became aware of impatient shuffling in the queue behind her, but this was important.

"I think he dropped his wallet. I've been trying to find him, or see if he's in regularly at least," Julia lied.

"Right," the woman said. "Yeah he was in last week. It's his usual time but he's only here every couple of weeks or so. You could try next week. Or I can take the wallet if you want?"

"No, that's okay," Julia said quickly, tapping her card and piling her shopping into her bag as fast as she could. The last thing she needed was being barred from here as well due to suspicious behaviour.

"Thanks for your help. Goodbye." Julia snatched her bag up and walked briskly towards the automated doors to the car park.

* * *

Julia knelt on her haunches staring into the oven. It seemed a fairly pointless endeavour. The cake inside just looked like a cake and she was going to take it out after thirty minutes, when the recipe said it would be done.

But she'd seen them do this on *Bake Off* on the telly and Sally was mooching back and forth past the doorway occasionally so she wanted to look like she knew what she was doing.

Her mind began to wander to the case. Mr Peabody's alibi had certainly checked out. Not that she'd ever been in serious doubts about that. She wondered just how many financial victims Beatrice Campbell had left in her wake.

Sally's voice stirred her from her train of thought. "Shouldn't you be taking that out?" she said.

"Oh, go away, Sally. Shoo," Julia said, snapping the tea towel at her.

Her friend obliged and disappeared back out of the kitchen, but she was right. The faint smell of burning was just beginning to fill the room. Muttering under her breath, Julia opened the oven door, ducking back from the blast of hot air, and used the tea towel to retrieve the cake.

The top was a dark brown. A very dark brown in fact. As Julia poked at it experimentally and watched it flake away she might even have conceded that it could be termed black.

Chapter 7

Julia climbed the steps leading up from the high street and unlocked the front door of the bookshop, scooping up the post from the black-and-white tiled floor of the entrance hall and opening the door to the shop floor with her hip.

Letting the letters fall down onto the counter, she retrieved a thermos of coffee from her handbag and unscrewed the lid. Taking a sip she unfolded the top letter from where it had been bent in half by the postman to fit it through the letter box and smoothed the crease out before opening it.

Her eyes skimmed down the page, settling on Mr Peabody's signature at the bottom and she muttered a brief curse at his name.

A business rates increase at the end of the month. Could they do that? She sighed and supposed that they could. Add that to the pile then, along with the increasing prices from their suppliers and the soaring heating costs. Maybe Ronald had it right keeping the heating so low his employees could see their breath in the winter. Did customers need to be warm? Who knew, maybe the cold would encourage them to buy more and browse less.

The bell over the door tinkled, rousing Julia from her thoughts. They weren't technically open yet and she hadn't flipped the sign. But Mr Peabody's letter was a stark reminder, as if she needed it, that they couldn't afford to turn paying customers away so she looked up with her best smile, which quickly melted away.

"Oh, it's you," Julia said.

"No, it isn't. I'm not here," Jones said. His tone was mock serious and he slipped quickly into the shop, closing the door behind him. His eyes darted furtively from side to side, scanning between the shelves.

Julia folded up the letter with the news about the increased rates and shoved it into a drawer under the counter. "Look, if you're here to make fun then I'm really not in the mood," she said.

"I'm not here to make fun," Jones said.

Despite this, as he made his way up to the counter his eyes were still darting about in an exaggerated fashion. He leaned one elbow on the counter with performative nonchalance, his back half-turned to Julia as though unaware of her presence. One hand dipped inside the pocket of his suit jacket and came out clutching a memory stick which he let fall onto the top of the counter before he straightened back upright.

"Remember, I was never here," he said without turning, and headed back out of the exit.

Julia scowled after him as he left and then picked up the USB stick. Whatever it was, it had better be useful. If this was his idea of a joke she was going to have words with him via Mark.

She retrieved the work laptop from its locked cupboard in the backroom and opened it up on the counter, waiting patiently while it gradually whirred into life. Then she stuck the memory stick into the side.

The drive contained only a single audio file. Julia craned over the counter to double-check for approaching customers. Satisfied that no one was about to batter the door down demanding stacks of books, she clicked play on the file.

'Hello, 999, what is your emergency?' the laptop said as it played the file back.

There was the sound of rasping breathing. Strangled breathing, Julia realized. This was the 999 call Beatrice Campbell had made, presumably after her killer had left her for dead.

'999, what is your emergency please?' the operator enquired again.

The rasping filtered back in, stronger this time. And then a single word. 'Cutty'.

'Can you repeat that please? Hello? Hello?'

The operator continued for a few more attempts but there was no response. Beatrice had breathed her last.

Julia cocked her head and listened intently as she played it back. Something about the recording was bothering her, but she couldn't put her finger on exactly what.

The bell rang over the door, making Julia jump. An elderly couple was making their way in, and Julia quickly hit stop on the recording and snatched the memory stick back out of the port, dropping it into her handbag for later. She sent out a silent wave of thanks to Jones as she flipped the lid shut on the laptop. So he was proving useful after all.

"Hello." Julia turned her attention to the couple and did her best to push the recording out of her mind for the time being. "Let me know if I can help you with anything."

"Just having a browse, thank you, dear," the woman said.

"The bus is late again, you see," her partner added.

Julia did her best to keep smiling as the couple made their way slowly over to the shelves in front of the counter. Who knew, maybe she'd be lucky and they'd buy something.

She headed over to turn the sign around and officially open. Just as she got back to the counter her phone chimed gently and she pulled it from her handbag. Her eyes lit up. Beatrice's nephew, Tony, had replied to her message.

Hi. What is it you wanted to know?

Blunt and to the point, but then he was responding to a complete stranger online.

'Can we meet in person?' she asked.

She still couldn't discount the possibility that Beatrice's murder had been personal, rather than ultimately motivated by the embezzlement, and so far Tony seemed to be her only relative in the area. Without any children of her own, perhaps Beatrice would have passed her money onto him?

At any rate, Julia wanted to gauge the man's reaction rather than rely on the relatively sterile medium of online messaging.

Julia held her breath as she waited for him to respond. There was nothing for a few moments and she was just starting to wonder if Tony had decided to ignore her out of hand, when little dots began to bubble actively in the chat as he typed.

OK. I'm in the King's Barrow area later today. Where do you want to meet?

Julia paused for a moment with her fingers poised. Somewhere public would be better. If the man was involved in his aunt's death somehow, then she needed to meet somewhere safe.

The Barley Mow?

Safe as houses. Yes, there were a few gossips there. Sally for one. But everyone there knew Julia and would look out for her if anything did go awry.

OK.

Now it was settled, it flashed through Julia's mind just how many people she'd met round the Barley Mow who had tried to kill her. But that was highly unlikely to happen again.

Another message appeared on her phone screen.

4pm OK? Will be passing by.

It would mean closing the shop a bit early. But this was important, and it didn't seem like hordes of book-buyers were going to press into the shop an hour before closing. She glanced up again at the couple who were doing their best to disorganize the fiction shelves.

OK. See you then.

* * *

The sun shone. Cow parsley burst abundantly from the verge beside the road, separating the tarmac from the shallow waters of the rhyne.

With the fields stretching away on the far bank, happily grazed by a herd of shaggy-haired brown cows underneath an azure blue sky, the scene should have been one to lift hearts.

But the walk brought up uncomfortable memories for Julia. In the past her sleuthing had led to more than one unsettling encounter along here and she would have preferred not to make the trip alone. Even Rumpkin would have provided some good moral support, although she doubted many determined assailants would be put off by him.

Coming straight from closing the shop, and with Mark unreachable on his worksite, neither her dog nor her boyfriend were options, so she found herself heading down the lane alone. She strode along as quickly as she could, feeling sweat start to prickle under her shirt as she marched.

Before too long she rounded the dogleg bend in the road and the Barley Mow came into view. Its cheerful sign was swinging high above, advertising the pub and also providing a perch for a pair of blackbirds.

The pub itself was a sprawling building under a thatched roof. The whitewash on its walls had faded over the years, lending it a feeling of permanence and belonging. The gravel car park which surrounded it on two sides was rather bare, even as the fields beyond burst into colour. The landlord, Ivan, was not much of a gardener.

He was, however, a shrewd businessman and knew how to make money when he needed to.

Behind the pub, a couple of hundred yards back, on the site of the old coach house, four new homes were under construction. The shell of them had gone up at an impressive rate and they stood roofless and windowless on the edge of the fields.

The bright-yellow, mud-encrusted construction vehicles had taken over the section of car park nearest the new builds and gone on to create their own parking in the churned-up ground alongside them as well. However, despite the number of vehicles, the builders themselves were nowhere to be seen.

A burst of laughter came drifting from one of the open windows of the pub, perhaps answering Julia's question.

Evidently Ivan wasn't paying by the day if that was the case.

Crossing over the gravel, Julia lifted the latch and stepped into the familiar surrounds of the parlour. It was a low room with small windows, making it dark even on days like today when the sun streamed down outside. Flagstones, well-worn over the years, covered the floor and tables lined the walls. Most of them were occupied, around half with what appeared to be the construction crew. Beers in hand, Julia hoped they'd finished for the day. Ivan, she supposed, would at least be happy they were pouring the wages he provided back into his pub.

The stools had been cleared from in front of the bar at the far end of the room, and Sally was standing on top of a short metal stepladder, tacking a string of bunting into the blackened oak beam that normally sported saddle ornaments.

It seemed the fever of the fête was catching here too.

Julia made another visual sweep of the room but it didn't seem that Tony had arrived yet. Checking her phone, she was still a few minutes early.

She made her way up to the bar, standing next to the ladder, and craned to look up at Sally.

"Drink, please," Julia said, relishing the opportunity to boss her friend about.

Sally looked down at her, hands aloft. She had a mouthful of tacks which prevented any immediate rebuttal. Switching the string of the bunting into one hand, she managed to remove the tacks with the other.

"Get it yourself," she said.

"I don't work here anymore," Julia said.

"And do I look like that bothers me?" Sally said.

Julia smiled and called out towards the back of the pub, holding Sally's eye while she did so. "Ivan! Sally's being unhelpful."

Sally glared down from her perch. "I can't believe you did that," she hissed.

Julia smiled sweetly and rocked on her heels.

Soon there was the sound of footsteps from the corridor behind the bar and Ivan emerged through the low door, stooping his tall frame to get under.

"What's she done now?" he sighed, wiping his hands on the apron that protected his immaculately starched shirt.

"She won't get me a drink," Julia said.

Sally waved the bunting string, the half-dozen or so triangular flags that she'd already attached jiggling perilously overhead. "I can only do one thing at a time," she said.

"And that thing should be serving me," said Julia.

Ivan shook his head at the two of them. "Can't you two play nicely?"

"No," they replied in unison.

"Fine," Ivan said, taking a step forward to the edge of the bar. "What are you having, Julia?"

"A small orange juice, please," she said.

"Wonderful, now I can retire," Ivan said, producing a glass bottle from the half-fridge under the bar and giving it a shake before pouring it.

Julia looked over her shoulder but there was still no Tony, so she turned her attention back to Ivan.

"I see you're getting ready for the fête then," she said.

"Oh, yes," Ivan said enthusiastically. "Practically mandatory, what with the pub's history."

That was lost on Julia. "What, because it was here during the war?" she ventured.

Ivan slumped slightly. "No, because this was where the rescue party set out from."

"Was it?" Julia said. That was news to her.

"Yes," Ivan replied. "The Home Guard were posted here on duty when the downed plane was spotted and this was where they headed out from. I've asked the council if they can have the parade finish here to honour that. So far they haven't got back to me though."

Julia brushed a stray strand of hair back. "Shouldn't the parade start from here, if this is where they set out from?"

Sally inserted the final tack into the beam and reversed down the steps.

"But then they wouldn't all end up here to spend their money," she said.

Ivan glared. "Enough of that," he said.

"What do you think?" Sally said, looking up at the bunting.

"I'm sure it's fine," Ivan said without bothering to move from behind the bar. "Now get back over here and start doing your job again."

With that he disappeared back into the staff corridor.

Julia looked up, appraisingly at the bunting. "It's a little wonky," she said.

"The whole pub's wonky," Sally said, folding the ladder up and depositing it behind the bar.

Julia heard the parlour door open, and she turned to see Tony stepping inside. She recognized him from his online picture, but he looked different in person. He was taller than she expected, and his dark hair was longer than it looked in his profile picture. He was blinking as his eyes adjusted to the dim lighting, and she saw him searching the room. She gave him a wave.

He made his way over to the bar, the sound of his footfalls lost in the conversation of the tables. Well that was good, a little background noise provided some privacy, in its way.

Julia studied Tony as they shook hands. He looked nervous and a little pale. She supposed that it had been a difficult period for him. Even agreeing to meet someone investigating the case indicated that he had nothing to hide, she supposed. Certainly, he had no obligation to see her if he did.

As Sally poured him a lemonade, Julia spotted that the little table tucked away by the hearth was free and she led Tony over to it.

She pulled her notebook out and flipped to the first unused page. It was depressingly near the start. She hadn't uncovered much, she thought.

"Sorry I'm a bit late, I had some trouble finding the pub," Tony said.

"That's all right, don't apologize. Thank you for coming to meet with me," she said as she settled onto one of the old wooden chairs, wobbly on the uneven flagstones of the floor.

"No, that's fine," he replied. "I was so shocked about what happened to Aunt Beatrice. Anything I can do to help. I gather her boss is the suspect."

Julia decided to make a clean breast of it. "It's actually Mr Cutty that I'm working for," she said.

Tony gave her a puzzled look as he tried to process this.

"He's maintaining his innocence, so we're exploring other avenues which the police aren't all that keen on doing," Julia explained. "In my experience, they like a nice, clean story. But the truth isn't always that simple."

"But if Mr Cutty didn't hurt my aunt then who did?" asked Tony.

"That's what I was hoping you might help me with," Julia said.

"I'm happy to help but I'm not sure there's much I can tell you," Tony said. "I hadn't seen Auntie in a little while. And she certainly wasn't the type to be making enemies."

Julia wondered briefly how many enemies her embezzlement scheme had made. "Well, I wanted to ask you a couple of questions about the doorbell that you bought her," she said.

"The JeevesDoor?" said Tony.

"I was told that you bought it for your aunt," Julia asked.

"Yes," he said. He sighed. "She was always saying that she didn't feel safe as a woman living alone where she did." He passed a hand over his face, looking like he was holding back a current of emotion. "I knew really she just wanted me to come visit more often and I kept brushing her off. Getting her the JeevesDoor was just one more way of doing that. I told her it would keep her safer. Really though I was just thinking it would save me some trips to see her."

Julia gave a short pause to let Tony gather himself a bit before she continued; it obviously hadn't been easy for the man losing his aunt. "It took a photo every time someone rang the doorbell and sent that to her phone, is that right?"

"Well really it uploads the photos to a cloud server under your account and then you can login to see them from your phone. But basically, yes," Tony said. He wiped once at his eyes but the emotion seemed to have passed.

He's obviously a techie, Julia thought, writing notes as she went. The whole contraption was meant to keep Beatrice safe, but it hadn't helped her in the end. A thought struck Julia.

"If the photos weren't sent directly to her phone, could I get a look at them?" she asked.

"I thought you already had them," said Tony. "The police said they'd seen her boss on them."

"Well the police have them," Julia said. "They aren't overly keen to share them with me."

"I see," Tony said. "I'm afraid I can't help you. You'd need the password that Auntie used when she set the account up."

Julia tapped at her teeth with the end of her pen. Another thought crossed her mind but she decided not to share it with Tony.

She scrawled a final line into her notebook and flipped it shut again.

"Thank you, Tony," she said, "you've been really helpful."

"If you find anything else about the missing money, you'll let me know, won't you?" Tony said, rising from his seat.

Julia looked up at him. "What do you mean?"

"I just can't believe that Aunt Beatrice was a thief. She didn't have it in her."

"Of course," Julia said. "Yes, of course."

She watched Tony return his glass to the bar and then duck his head under the beams as he headed for the door.

It was natural enough that he didn't want to believe his aunt had been an embezzler. But how well did he really know her? By his own admission, the two of them hadn't been close.

Julia put her notebook back into her bag and went up to find Sally at the bar. She wanted to give Tony a bit of time to leave before she followed.

* * *

Julia hurried upstairs to her room to fetch her laptop. Then she came down and searched for it in the living room. Despite Rumpkin's help, she didn't find it there either. Eventually she found it in Sally's room, open on her nightstand with a light dusting of foundation on the keys which she brushed off.

Rumpkin gave a satisfied yip and, happy with a job well done, he jumped up onto the forbidden temptation of Sally's bed and stamped round in circles on the duvet before hunkering down.

Julia watched the ritual. "Yeah, you sleep there, I think she deserves it." He would get shifted as soon as she got back from the Barley Mow, but in the meantime he could cover her bed in hairs for all Julia cared.

Laptop clutched under one arm, she headed back downstairs, threw herself into the armchair and pressed the on button. After locating the charger and plugging it in she tried again.

Finally, the screen lit up and Julia logged in and after a bit of searching found the website for JeevesDoor.

She was keen to get this done before Mark returned. She didn't know if what she was doing was technically illegal and she preferred not to know. At least this way Mark wasn't implicated in it, even if he was likely to be far more gung-ho about it than she was. Julia furrowed her brow. Perhaps Mark was rubbing off on her a bit too much.

Ronald had already provided Julia with Beatrice's email address as part of the file he'd put together. So now it was just a case of guessing her password. Her birthday followed by her street address didn't work, but Julia had success on the second attempt: her street address followed by her birthday. Dillon's information had proved to be spot on.

Once logged in, Julia was presented with a picture of a helpful-looking butler holding open a door, and underneath was a list of folders each with their own date, ending with the day Beatrice was killed.

Julia clicked on that folder and a handful of square photo thumbnails appeared on the screen. She clicked each one in turn.

First there was the postman. He was wearing a baseball cap and looking back the way he had come as he rang the bell, so his face was obscured. But it wasn't really him that Julia was interested in and she moved on to the next photo.

There was Ronald. The resolution wasn't great, but Julia could see that he was looking a bit red and flustered. Perhaps chapped from the wind, it had been a cold day. Or perhaps he hadn't calmed down as much as he claimed that he had.

She stuck her nose closer to the screen trying to see if the camera might have caught anyone else loitering at the bottom of the steps in the strip of tarmac that ran down the side of the supermarket. Julia sighed. There was nothing to see, as far as she could tell.

She went onto the next and final image for good measure. Two police constables, looking alert, their car visible in the background below them, the fierceness of the blue light on top washing out part of the frame. Presumably this was just moments before they broke the door in.

Julia was just studying the image when she heard the familiar sound of Mark's van pulling up on the street outside.

At the bottom of the screen was a little toolbar and she hit the large, pale-blue arrow that downloaded all of the images onto her own laptop. Who knew if she'd have access to this account again.

Mark opened the front door, calling hello over the top of the sofa as he pulled his jacket off, and Julia hastily shut the browser window down.

Mark made his way over to the armchair and placed a kiss on the top of Julia's head.

"How are you?" Julia asked him.

"Ah, another long day," he said as he collapsed down into the sofa beside Julia's seat. "What are you up to there?"

Julia bent over to her handbag on the floor next to the chair and pulled out the USB stick that Jones had given her. She held it up for Mark's inspection before plugging it into the laptop. "Listen to this," she said.

Mark craned forward, intently listening to the recording of the 999 call.

He shivered slightly as it finished. "I can't say that my day's improved any by hearing that," he said.

Julia played Beatrice's utterance of 'Cutty' back again. "Don't you think there's something strange about the way she says that?" Julia asked.

"Strange how?" said Mark.

"I can't put my finger on it. Just a little off?" Julia knew it sounded a bit feeble when she put it into words.

"She was being strangled at the time," Mark said.

Julia closed the laptop with a quiet bang. "I suppose you're right," she said.

"We have my dad to thank for getting that, do we?" said Mark, folding back into the sofa.

"Yes," said Julia.

Mark pulled a cushion up over his face. "Great. As though he wasn't smug enough already."

Chapter 8

Sally's car was home but there was no sign of her as Julia came in the front door after work the following day.

"Sally?" she called out.

"Kitchen," the reply came back.

Julia pushed the kitchen door open and stepped in.

The oven was empty, but it had been left ajar and Julia could feel the heat flowing from it, so it had obviously been in use recently. Sieves, spoons and mixing bowls covered the counters, not to mention several strata of flour and icing sugar.

All the signs of baking were there, but conspicuous in its absence was any actual cake.

"Where is it?" Julia asked.

Sally gave a saccharine smile as she stood filling the kettle with water. "It's a secret," she said. "Close your eyes and I'll get some."

Julia narrowed them rather than close them. "I'm not doing that," she said.

She peered round behind Sally in case she was concealing something on the counter.

There was no cake there but there was a splattered sheet of handwritten paper which must be the recipe.

Julia's hand darted for it, but Sally was quicker, snatching it away and shoving it into the pouch pocket of her baking apron.

"I want to see," Julia said.

"I said it's a secret," said Sally.

Julia glowered before stalking out of the room. She looked at Rumpkin as the animal appeared at her ankles. "You'd tell me, wouldn't you, boy?" she said, patting him roughly on the top of the head.

"Here." Julia hadn't heard Sally sneaking up and it made her jump.

When she turned around, her friend was holding out a small slice of cake, the same signature red, white and blue Britainberg which Julia had seen her preparing the other day.

"Is that all I'm getting?" Julia said, making a show of squinting at the morsel.

"Just open," Sally said.

Julia obliged.

Whatever her friend had changed since last time, Sally had improved on her own high standards. In fact, she had worked a positive miracle in that kitchen.

Apparently Julia's thoughts showed on her face, because Sally lit up into a smile. "Good, isn't it?"

Julia swallowed. "Passable, I guess."

"Passable, hm?"

Julia sighed. It was pointless to pretend, it wasn't as though Sally didn't already know how good it was. "Fine. It's amazing. More please."

"Nope."

Julia did her best to scowl, which proved difficult to do whilst licking her lips. "Maybe I'll bake one myself. What did you change?"

"I told you, it's a secret recipe," Sally said. "Besides, it's a bit advanced for you."

Julia gasped but before she could reply Sally had turned and flounced her way back into the kitchen.

Too advanced for her? Who did Sally think she was dealing with? When Julia won that bake-off she would enjoy seeing that smirk wiped straight off her friend's face.

And anyway, Julia was a budding detective now, she didn't need to see the recipe. What had gone into her mouth wasn't only delicious, it was also cold. It could only have come out of the fridge.

She flopped down into the armchair and allowed Rumpkin to climb up onto her lap. The game was well and truly afoot.

* * *

Sally had hidden the small bottles of food colouring, but not well enough. By kneeling precariously on the countertop, Julia had located them at the back of the top cupboard behind the paper cake cases.

It was a fine enough plan, relying on Julia's short stature and the fact the cake cases weren't being used, so logically nothing should be hidden behind them.

Once she had located the colouring, Julia had mixed up pastes that she was confident were the same colours Sally had used.

Then she'd discovered Sally's cake in the freezer, not the fridge as she'd initially expected. So the fondant holding the quarters together was some kind of ice cream.

Knowing Sally, she would have made her own, but Julia had got Mark to pick up a tub of white ice cream from the supermarket on his way back from work. She was confident it would taste just as good.

Now was the moment of truth, and Julia took her freshly assembled cake out of the freezer where it had been setting and placed it on the countertop.

She drew a large cake knife from the block and as neatly as she could manage cut a thick slice.

It looked wonderful. Almost indistinguishable from Sally's, except if you looked closely the fondant on the outside wasn't as neatly spread. But that was a detail Julia could fix when it came time to do the real thing.

She reached forward gingerly and picked the chill slice of cake up between thumb and forefinger.

As she did so the ice cream glue slid apart and the four quarters of the cake flopped in separate directions. One remained clutched in Julia's grasp but she watched helplessly as the other three peeled away, bounced off the edge of the counter and landed with a plop on the lino floor by her feet.

Rumpkin gave an excited woof and inserted his head between Julia's ankles in order to start lapping up the unexpected manna.

"Oh, you traitor," Julia said to the animal, but he paid her no attention.

Julia put the surviving quarter into her mouth and chewed thoughtfully. At least it tasted okay. She would be lying if she said it was as good as Sally's, but there was still time to experiment. And time to solve the consistency problem too, she thought as she looked at the rapidly disappearing cake on the floor.

Julia's ears pricked up and she thought she heard the sound of an engine outside, probably Sally returning from work.

Working hastily, Julia grabbed a slice of Sally's cake and concealed it by placing it in with her own. It would pay to have a reference slice for research and development, and Sally would never notice just one missing.

As the front door clattered open, Julia hurried to get both cakes back in the freezer and she swept the knife and cutting board into the sink just as she heard the front door slam.

"Hello there," Sally said, poking her head through the kitchen door. "What are you up to?"

"Just deciding what to have for dinner," Julia said, making a show of looking through the tin cupboard.

"Well can you be quick? I want to practise my bake before turning in," Sally said.

Julia gave a belaboured sigh. "Practise again? It's not that big a deal, Sally."

* * *

Julia saw Mrs Burns's head going past the shop window, a determined expression etched upon her face.

She quickly finished watering the spider plant – a cutting which Mark's mum had given her to 'brighten the place up a bit' – and hurried round the shelves towards the counter.

If Mrs Burns was here to buy up her baking selection again then that was just fine by her. Julia had restocked after Mrs Burns had cleared her out the other day and even managed to sell a couple of books to other bake-off hopefuls. So if Mrs Burns wanted to fruitlessly pour money into the shop's coffers then it didn't seem to harm anyone except Mrs Burns.

Julia laid her hands on the countertop and beamed pleasantly as Mrs Burns came in. As she saw what the woman was carrying though, Julia had to make an effort to fix her smile in place.

Mrs Burns was staggering in behind the stack of books she'd previously purchased. She placed them down just in front of Julia's nose with a weighty thump and then adjusted her spectacles.

"I'd like to return these books, please," Mrs Burns said.

Julia quickly looked up and down the spines in dismay. "All of them?" she asked, swallowing. It looked like Mrs Burns was returning the whole lot.

"Yes, all of them," said Mrs Burns.

Julia took the top one of the pile and peered at it. She'd already bought in the replacement, what would she do with two?

"Come on, I don't have all day to dally around," Mrs Burns said.

Julia sighed, ran the book through the scanner, and picked up the next one.

"This one has cocoa powder fingerprints on the cover," Julia said, holding it up for Mrs Burns to see.

Instead, Mrs Burns turned her face away, raising her nose to the ceiling. "It was like that when I bought it," she said. "I'd really urge you to take better care of your stock or you'll end up with no customers at all, I shouldn't wonder."

Julia's shoulders slumped, she really didn't have the energy to argue and she scanned the book through and picked up the next one.

She barely registered as Mrs Burns scooped up her refunded cash, put it into her purse, and without a word strode from the shop.

That had been the single biggest sale that Julia had made. In fact, it had probably been their most profitable day since their opening week. And now all the merchandise had been handed back by Mrs Burns. On top of which, Julia had duplicate stock on her hands. Not to mention that more than one of the returned items was smudged with flour and cocoa powder, rendering them unsellable.

Despondently, Julia picked up the baking book with Mrs Burns's fingerprints prominent on the glossy white cover and stuck it on the shelf underneath the till. Maybe she could make some use of it at home and then it wouldn't be a complete loss.

She was still ruminating on her sorry lot in life when the bell rang again. She forced herself out of her slump and sat upright on the stool, not really aware how much time she'd spent stewing. She did her best to smile.

The man who entered returned her smile and then some, flashing a row of pearly-white teeth. He was a young man, probably about Julia's age, and sharply dressed in a suit and tie. She had heard of people having a spring in their step before but the man positively bounced across the room to her.

"Hello," Julia said, studying the man carefully and gauging that he wasn't a typical Biddle Rhyne bookworm. "Can I help you?"

"You certainly can," the man said. He reached into his breast pocket with his thumb and forefinger and with a flourish withdrew a business card which he held aloft in front of Julia.

The man read it out to her even as she read the card herself. "Lionel Buckminster – Tammerick Property Services," he said. "I have a proposition for you, Miss Ford."

Julia lowered the business card and looked at the glowing face on the other side of the counter, unsure where this was headed.

"I have a client interested in purchasing this shop," Mr Buckminster said, making a sweeping movement with his arm to indicate the shelves behind him. "I know, of course, that the business will be very dear to you. But I'm hopeful we can find a price that will be acceptable to both parties."

Julia was taken aback. As much as she loved the bookshop, unless her sales changed course dramatically it was only going to lose money, especially with the rate rise coming up.

The shop was as much Mark's as hers, financially. And he'd put in a monumental effort to see it into existence at all. But he'd probably be just as happy with a pay day as she was, if not more.

"Possibly," Julia managed to mutter back, bamboozled by the man's enthusiasm.

Taking a pen from his suit, he clicked it open and wrote a number down in small, neat writing on the back of his business card. "This was my client's opening offer" – he leaned in and lowered his voice – "although between you and me they might be willing to negotiate."

Julia looked at the number on the card and blinked. Someone was even more keen to run a bookshop than she had been. Hopefully they would have more luck than she had. Warming to the idea now, Julia had images in her mind of wandering into the store, coffee in hand. Casting a wistful eye over the shelves and thinking back to her time at the helm. Maybe even giving the occasional pointer to the new owner. An owner who might want a part-time employee to help run the place, now that business had picked up under their stewardship.

She forced herself back into the here and now. "We do have a long-term rental agreement with the council," she said.

"At Tammerick Property Services we've dealt with Biddle Council on multiple occasions," he said. "We have an excellent working relationship. I'm confident that we can get them to make an allowance. More than confident, in fact. I'm certain."

Julia couldn't help looking again at the figure written on the card. "I'll need to talk to my partner about it," she said. "He's an owner too."

"Well yes, no problem, Miss Ford," Mr Buckminster said. "You do that. I'll call back in a few days and see where you're at with your thinking. Or call the number on my card, I'll be happy to talk you through everything."

With that, Mr Buckminster gave a little nod of the head, somehow evoking a tip of a non-existent hat, and bounced back towards the door, striking up a whistling tune as he went.

* * *

Julia's phone rang, and she hurried downstairs to answer it.

"Hi Julia," Ronald's voice said. He sounded strained, understandably. "I've got a new lead for you from Dillon. Another of Beatrice's victims."

Julia did her best not to sound out of breath from her dash down the stairs. "What have you got?" she asked, scrabbling around on the coffee table looking for a pen.

"A man named Brad Moore. I don't know much about him, I never met him myself. He was a relatively recent client, but it seems that his account got tapped all the same. He runs a small graphic design company. The sums aren't huge in the scheme of things, but relative to the size of the business they probably stung."

"I can check him out," Julia said, and wrote down the rest of the details Ronald had before she hung up.

She looked at the clock and sighed. Almost four. The bookshop closed early on Wednesdays, along with the rest of Biddle Rhyne's high street. She was meant to be seeing Mark when he finished so they could walk their dogs together. It looked like that plan had gone out the window now.

This lead had better be worth it, Julia thought, as she dialled Mark's number.

Chapter 9

Julia drove the car through the winding country lanes. So far she'd been fortunate enough not to meet anything coming in the other direction. Mark sat beside her in the passenger seat peering through the windscreen looking for their turnoff. Ronald had given them the address but the map on Julia's phone didn't show anything there.

Sally had reluctantly let Julia borrow the car and even more reluctantly agreed she could take Rumpkin and Mark's Labrador, Manny, in the boot. The plan now was to walk the dogs after visiting Mr Moore. Even Julia had to admit that it wasn't the most professional thing for an investigator to pull up with a car full of dogs, so she was hoping she could park somewhere a bit out of the way where the animals wouldn't be too obvious.

After picking Mark up, Julia had told him about Mr Buckminster's offer, on behalf of Tammerick Property Services, to purchase the shop from them. Since then he had mostly been silent for the drive, watching the countryside moving past.

Julia sighed. "I thought you'd be happy to be rid of the shop," she said.

Mark looked at her. Keeping her eyes on the road, Julia could only see him out of the edge of her vision, but he looked a bit taken aback by that.

"I was happy to get that shop going," he said. "It was mostly my idea, remember? I thought it was what you wanted."

"It was," Julia said. "I mean, it is. But it's hardly paying its way, is it?"

Mark gave a shrug and looked back out through the windscreen again. "We're not at risk of being on the breadline just yet," he said.

"I guess not," Julia said, although she knew that really it was only Mark's painting that prevented that.

Their conversation was curtailed as they rounded a corner. "I think there's a house up there," Mark said, straining against his seat belt to see round the bend.

Happily Julia was only going about fifteen miles per hour so she made the exit easily enough.

The turn-off did appear to be leading to a house: Julia could catch flashes of it through the hedges. After driving down the narrow lane for about a minute they arrived at the entrance. The hedge changed into a low wall of red brick with a gate set into it, luckily left open. The bricks gleamed crimson in the sunshine. Judging by how pristine they were, it looked like the place was newly built which might explain its absence on the map. There was a sign, also shiny and new-looking, fixed into the brickwork on one side of the gate. But rather unhelpfully it had no address or house name, it was just advertising 'Graphic Design Solutions' with some stylized writing and an artistic picture of a tree on it.

The car's suspension rocked as it crossed a cattle grid just beyond the gate. A narrow strip of tarmac serpentined its way through lush grass bordered by tall bushes. Julia kept alert for any grazing animals as she drove but she didn't spot any.

The tarmac led them to a house, the front of which was glass from top to bottom. Presumably it was designed to let the inhabitants look out over the meadowy grounds attached to the house.

Julia pulled up in the paved yard outside the house, sticking to the far end where she hoped the dogs would remain unseen.

It wasn't to be. There was a smaller building alongside the house, also glass-fronted. As the car came to a halt, the door of the outbuilding opened and a man stepped out and came striding over the yard towards them. From the boot of the car, Rumpkin and Manny began yowling, feeling they should be let free.

Julia snapped at the dogs to be quiet, but they paid her no attention, each trying to outdo the other in volume. Muttering curses at them, Julia slipped out of the car just in time for the man to reach them.

He was tall, with greying hair that flew out, unbrushed, in all directions, billowing in the wind. Despite the early spring chill, he wore only a T-shirt, showing the sinewy muscle of his arms. He loomed over Julia, coming just one pace closer than was comfortable.

"Can I help you?" he asked pointedly.

Julia swallowed. It seemed that he might have moved out here for the peace and quiet and didn't take too kindly to visitors turning up unannounced.

"Are you Mr Moore?" Julia asked.

"Yes," the man replied, no more friendly than before. "But if you're after graphic design work I'm afraid I'll have to ask you to call the office in advance. I'm very busy right now."

"Actually I'm here about your account with Miss Beatrice Campbell," Julia said.

Mr Moore squinted at her. "What do you mean? That's a police matter, and you aren't police, unless I'm much mistaken."

"You're right, we're not police," Julia said, indicating to herself and Mark who had made his way around the car to stand next to her. "My name is Julia Ford. We're actually working for Mr Cutty."

Mr Moore screwed his face up. "Working for Mr Cutty? Here to try and do some damage control, are you? Well, it won't work. That was my money, and I want to see every last penny of it returned."

"You don't quite understand," Julia said, as mildly as she could, resisting the urge to slip back inside the safety of the car. "Are you aware that Miss Campbell was murdered?"

"I heard," said Mr Moore. Neither his face nor his tone gave much away.

"We're just trying to establish the facts around what happened," Julia said. "Are you able to tell us where you were that night?"

Mr Moore exploded in a sudden bout of laughter that made Julia jump.

"It's like that, is it? Well, I could have been on the moon for all that it matters to you. I don't have to answer your questions and I'm not going to."

"It's just it would be helpful if–" Julia began, but Mr Moore cut her off.

He waved a hand back at the gates. "Be off with you, and take those mutts with you before they scare the sheep to death."

Julia couldn't help glancing around and again noting the complete absence of livestock, but she gave a meek dip of the head and opened the car door.

Mr Moore stood with his arms folded and eyes glaring, watching as Julia slowly spun the car around in a tight circle and headed back the way they'd come in. She caught a glimpse of him in the rear-view mirror as they went, still standing there, staring after them.

"He was friendly," Mark said.

Julia bit her lip and focused back on the road as she went back over the cattle grid and onto the lane.

"I guess we were accusing him of murder, in a roundabout sort of way," she said. She supposed that she needed to work on her questioning techniques.

"If you have nothing to hide, though," Mark said, "if he had an alibi he could have just given it to us and we'd have been out of his hair."

"I suppose so," Julia said, switching up a gear as the lane straightened out. "We'll need another way of finding out where he was when Beatrice was killed."

"And what if he was our killer?" Mark asked. "Then we won't find anything."

That was true, Julia supposed. They could rule people out, but ruling anyone in was going to be much harder with the evidence that they had. She mulled this over as the countryside flowed past on either side.

"Where are you heading for anyway?" said Mark. "I thought we were going up Pagan's Hill."

"Oh, right," Julia said, looking for a place to turn the car around.

* * *

It was getting dark when they arrived home a few hours later. Julia backed the car up on the narrow driveway that ran alongside their rather neglected garden, the grass and accompanying weeds rising up to knee height and still waiting for their first mow of the spring season.

As she got out of the car, Julia noticed that it was rather muddier now than when she'd borrowed it. But it was forecast to rain later that day so perhaps she'd get away with it.

She was just making her way round the side of the vehicle to release the two dogs from the back when she paused. The window next to the front door was slightly ajar.

"What's wrong?" Mark asked, noticing her expression as he squeezed out next to the fence and shut the passenger side door.

Julia didn't reply but hurried quietly over to the window, beckoning Mark to follow.

"This wasn't open when we left," Julia said in a harsh whisper.

As Mark inspected the window, Julia put her ear to the door and listened. Admittedly the window was only open a crack, but if someone had entered they could easily have pulled it to behind them.

"Are you sure?" Mark asked.

"Yes."

"Or Sally might be home," he suggested.

Julia chewed her bottom lip. "Possibly. She was meant to be working until late though."

Julia tapped on the peeling paintwork. It was an old wooden window frame, long overdue for replacement, and flaky and misshapen in many places. But there was definitely a groove alongside the catch, which looked like someone had worked it open with a screwdriver.

She looked back down the driveway to the street. They were largely hidden behind the car now, but without it they would be in full view. Would someone be brazen enough to break in like that? Admittedly it was a quiet enough street in a quiet enough village. Not exactly a lot of passers-by to stumble upon any would-be thief if they were quick.

Mark put his hand in his pocket for his spare key but Julia put a restraining hand on his wrist. "They could still be in there," she whispered.

"Even better," said Mark, "we can catch them in the act and see who it is."

Julia thought for a moment. "It must be Mr Moore," she said.

"What makes you say that?"

"We questioned him earlier today and now someone's broken in. I don't believe in coincidences like that."

Mark frowned. "And what would he be looking for?"

"He wants to see what evidence we've collected. There must be something he doesn't want us to know."

"But we haven't found anything on him," Mark pointed out.

"He doesn't know that," said Julia.

Mark conceded the point. "Fine. Look, I'll text Dad and get him here, but we need to see if anyone's in there."

The dogs yipped impatiently in the back of the car. Julia toyed briefly with the idea of bringing them in for protection, but neither animal had proved very useful in this capacity in the past so she left them to their protests.

"All right," she said to Mark.

Between the car pulling up and the ruckus the dogs were making, if the thief was still inside then they must surely have realized by now that Julia had returned. If they hadn't already fled over the back fence, then the thought must be crossing their mind soon.

Mark turned the key in the door and slowly let it swing open to reveal the downstairs of the house.

Julia followed him in, peering over his shoulder at the gloomy living room and straining her ears for any hint of movement about the house.

Mark stretched under the stairs and came back holding Julia's umbrella. It wasn't the sturdiest of objects and only had a flimsy-looking plastic handle, but she had seen Sally drive an assailant away with an umbrella before so she didn't argue.

Together they advanced cautiously round the side of the armchair and into the living room. There were no obvious signs of ransacking. Nothing had been torn from the shelves or knocked over. But Julia could swear some of the drawers at the bottom of the bookshelf were open a crack when they hadn't been before.

"Let's check the rest of the house," Mark whispered.

The kitchen was in a state of disarray from Sally's morning baking, but again there was nothing obviously out of place, and the kitchen drawers hadn't been turned out.

Upstairs was a similar story. All the valuables were still in place: jewellery, TVs, Sally's tablet.

Mark began to relax. "It doesn't look like anything was taken. Maybe the window was just left open by mistake," he said.

Julia shot him a look. "If it was Mr Moore then he wasn't here to nick my necklaces, was he? He was seeing what evidence we had, he wouldn't have to remove anything."

Her eyes widened as a thought struck her. "My laptop," she said.

Mark pointed back towards Sally's room. "It's on the desk in there," he said.

"Exactly," said Julia. "Why would I ever leave it there?"

She hurried back into Sally's room with Mark following after her.

Julia looked at the desk. Her laptop tended to move all around the house and be in the last place she would think to look for it. But she never set herself down to work at Sally's desk, unless she was printing something. "Someone's been using it," Julia said.

"Probably Sally then," said Mark.

"I hope not. I warned her about that! No, someone's been in here and I bet it's Mr Moore wanting to see what I had on there."

"You have a password on it though, right?" Mark asked.

"Yes, of course," Julia said. "I'm not Beatrice."

Julia sat down on the little swivel chair and opened up the laptop. The screen instantly came to life displaying her emails. "Of course, I don't always remember to lock the screen," she muttered.

She stared at the screen and tried to think what they would have found if someone had trawled through it. The 999 call, the CCTV stills and the photos from the doorbell.

Of course there was nothing on there that would incriminate Mr Moore. That was Julia's problem.

Unless there was something in those files she hadn't spotted.

Well, if that was the case then it stood to reason that Mr Moore would need to cover his tracks.

And, if Julia hadn't missed anything, then Mr Moore would know she wasn't close on his trail yet and could keep stonewalling.

She leaned back on the chair. She needed to keep a watch on Mr Moore, and she needed to do it subtly.

* * *

Julia poked at the window pane, double-checking that it was shut securely.

"Leave it, it's fine," Mark said.

Julia ignored him and gave it one more poke of the finger. Through the window she could see the muddy car. The predicted rainfall had never materialized. The sun was setting now, casting long shadows down their street. As she gave the window one final poke to test it was shut properly, Julia saw a movement at the end of the driveway.

"Finally," Julia said, pulling open the front door.

Jones trudged up the driveway, hands in his suit pockets. His face serious, he gave Julia a look as he arrived on her doorstep. "I'm sorry to hear about what happened," he said.

Julia folded her arms across her chest as she stood back to let Jones in. "You took your time getting here," she said.

Jones clicked his tongue. "I was working," he said.

"There was a crime right here," Julia said, "you could have been working here."

Jones gave a heavy sigh. "Well, I'm here now."

"Yes," said Julia. "I think you need to dust for prints."

She saw the unenthused expression on his features. "What?" she said.

"Julia, do you honestly think that someone with a criminal record broke in here today and was rifling through your things?" he said.

"They might have," Julia replied firmly.

"And if that was the case, they didn't bother to wear gloves?" the detective asked.

"Maybe they knew you wouldn't bother to collect fingerprints," Julia said.

"And they'd have been right."

"But if you do collect fingerprints then you would find them," said Julia.

"An elaborate double bluff, you think?" said Jones.

"It's possible."

Jones's broad shoulders slumped. "Fine. Fine. Julia, I'll dust the window and the laptop for prints. But you have to promise you'll call Freiland and report this through the official channels."

The two of them stood staring at one another.

"Julia," Jones prompted.

"All right, fine," Julia said, leaving the policeman to dust the window, and heading into the living room to retrieve her phone.

Julia dialled the station number, a thing she sadly knew by heart now, and asked for Freiland. There was a buzzing sound as she was put on hold. While she waited she hovered over Jones's shoulder watching him work with the fingerprint kit.

Apparently he was done a moment later because he began to climb the stairs to dust the laptop. Just as Julia was about to follow him up she heard Freiland's voice down the line.

"DI Freiland speaking."

"Detective. It's me, Julia Ford." She began pacing a circuit of the living room.

A sigh came down the phone line. It was oddly reminiscent of Jones's. "What is it, Miss Ford?"

"I've got a suspect in the Beatrice Campbell murder," Julia said.

There was a long pause on the other end before Freiland spoke again. "I suppose I would technically be negligent if I didn't ask who," she said.

"Mr Brad Moore," Julia said.

"Mmhmm." Freiland's tone was disinterested. "And what makes you say this?"

"He was one of the victims of Miss Campbell's embezzlement," Julia said.

"I see," Freiland replied. "And did he discover this fact before or after Miss Campbell was killed?"

Julia hesitated. "As far as I know, after," she said.

"Right."

"But he might have found out before and not told anyone," Julia added quickly.

"Yes," said Freiland. "There's no surer way to recover your embezzled money than not alerting anyone and offing the person who did it."

Julia sighed now. "There's more. He refused to tell us where he was the night Miss Campbell was killed."

"I don't blame him."

"And he broke into my house today," Julia said.

"He did?"

"Yes."

"And how did he find out where you lived?" Freiland asked.

Julia paused, but only for a moment. "That's surely easy enough. After all, I found out where he lived, didn't I?"

"Miss Ford, what have you been up to?"

The detective's tone was stern, but it washed right over Julia. Her mind was whirring now and she spoke more to herself than to Freiland. "Unless it was one of the other suspects we've been questioning, of course."

The voice on the other end of the phone was louder this time, ensuring it got Julia's full attention.

"As I've said to you before, I need to insist that you stop this investigation of yours before someone gets hurt. Or more likely, really, really annoyed. Now, I've made a note of what you've told me and I'll add it to the file. Which technically covers me if you follow this up, unlike if I just throw the note in the bin which is sorely tempting.

But honestly, I'd advise you just to stick to selling books. Now, good evening."

The line went dead and Julia dropped the phone defeatedly onto the cushions of the sofa.

As she did so the front door handle turned and Sally came in. At Julia's request, Charlie had driven her back from work that evening.

She came over and wrapped Julia up in a hug. Her skin was fragrant from the cold air.

"Sounds like you've had quite a rough day," Sally said as she released Julia.

Julia nodded. "There was someone in the house while we were out, I'm certain of it."

"But they didn't take anything?" Sally said.

"I don't think so."

"Hm…" Sally looked thoughtful, absently casting an eye over the living room for anything missing. "I'll check later."

"I think they were looking for something," Julia said.

Sally gasped. "Like my secret recipe," she said.

"No, not like that." Julia felt her hands balling into fists and made them relax. "I mean like evidence from the case."

"I didn't realize you had any," Sally said, turning her back on Julia before she could level her full scowl at her.

"Unless you've been using my laptop?" Julia asked.

Sally shook her head, blonde curls tumbling. "Of course not," she said. "Speaking of borrowing things though, the car's filthy. What have you been doing with it?"

She was spared from replying because there were heavy footsteps on the stairs and Jones came plodding down them.

"Are you all finished?" Julia asked him.

He gave a sharp nod. "Yes. Well there were some prints on the window and the laptop. Of course I'll need to exclude everyone here," he said.

"And then you can run them through the database?" said Julia.

"Yes, and then I can run them through the database," Jones said. "In the meantime, I suggest you stay well away from Mr Moore."

Julia scowled. "You sound just like Freiland," she said.

"Well, stopped clocks and all that. Just occasionally she gets things right," Jones said. "The chances are you'll be harassing an innocent man. And if that's not the case then he's someone highly dangerous and I certainly wouldn't recommend harassing him."

When Julia didn't reply, Jones continued. "So you will stay away, won't you?"

"Yes," Julia lied. She needed to see what Mr Moore got up to that night. But she would be careful. He would never know she was there.

* * *

"Turn the headlights back on," Mark said, reaching across Julia for the knob on the dashboard.

Julia swatted at his hand. "What if Mr Moore sees us coming?" she said.

Mark swore. "For pity's sake, Julia, it's pitch black here. You're going to drive us into a hedge. And besides, he's hardly going to know it's us just from a pair of headlights driving past the end of his road, is he?"

Something solid and branchlike brushed the side of the car and begrudgingly Julia turned the dipped beams on and then hauled hard on the steering wheel to navigate around a particularly stealthy tree which had crept up on her.

A lay-by came into sight as they rounded the corner.

"Maybe we should stop here anyway," Julia said, slowing Sally's car down.

"Fine by me," Mark muttered.

"No need to be like that," Julia said as she came to a halt and pulled on the handbrake. She glared at Mark. "What are you doing?"

He paused with one hand inside the glovebox. "Getting the torch," he said.

Julia flipped the glovebox shut again, causing Mark to quickly retract his fingers. "No way. Mr Moore will definitely see us if we bimble around with torches on, it's pitch dark out there."

"Exactly," Mark said.

"No torches," Julia said firmly, getting out of the car.

They walked the last half-mile or so in silence, stumbling occasionally when there was a rut in the lane or a branch lying across the tarmac. It seemed the hedges had been trimmed down there recently.

Eventually they reached the low brick wall that marked the start of Mr Moore's property. Julia crept along it.

"Look," she whispered. "The gate's open."

Mark looked at the yawning space where the gates weren't. "I'm beginning to think Mr Moore may not be the criminal mastermind we figured him to be," he said.

Julia went to slap him with the back of her fingers but in the blackness she missed him.

She looked through the gateway down the long driveway. Lights were shining in the glass frontage of the house, although it was too far away for them to discern anything more than that. Interestingly, Julia noted there was a warm orange square of light coming from the studio as well.

"Someone's working late," Julia muttered to herself.

"What did you say?" asked Mark.

"Nothing. Never mind. Come on, we need to get closer," Julia said.

Dropping down into a low crouch, Julia crept forward through the gateway.

She was just at the far edge when a shape moved across the darkness in front of her and she felt a warm, sticky breath on her fingertips.

Julia let out a shrill scream. "Run, Mark!" she shouted. "He's got a guard dog."

She felt Mark's hand clamp onto her through her coat and pull her back towards the road. "Come on," he implored her.

Julia took one stumbling step backwards and landed on her backside. "I can't," she said. "My foot's stuck in the cattle grid."

There was a low bleating sound and an amorphous, fluffy shape sidled across in front of her and disappeared into the lawns.

Julia laid a hand onto her beating heart. "It was just a sheep," she said.

Her relief was short-lived because from the direction of the house she heard a door slam and a beam of torchlight came sweeping out, making its way down the drive towards them.

"He's heard us," Mark said. "Hurry."

Julia scrambled upright and gave a jerk of her leg and grunted. "I can't, Mark, I'm really stuck," she said.

"Pull harder," Mark replied, grabbing hold under her armpits and tugging her backwards.

Julia gasped as the grating of the cattle grid bit into her ankle but then there was a sliding sensation and she felt her shoe come loose, freeing her foot.

She tumbled back into Mark's arms.

"Come on," he said, pulling her backwards.

Julia gawped at the torch coming closer through the darkness, the sound of footsteps on tarmac audible now as well. She allowed Mark to heave her back onto the road and he threw himself down behind the wall just as the footsteps came clanging over the cattle grid, dragging Julia down next to him.

"Who's there?" a voice demanded.

Julia tried to still her breathing. The torch swept one way and then the other down the road as she crammed herself flat against the brick wall, feeling Mark squashed against her.

The torch beam swung around once more and then turned, leaving the road in darkness again. There was a muted grumbling as the footsteps retreated back over the gateway.

Julia looked to Mark, unable to see him in the pitch dark of the night. "Too close," she whispered.

"Way too close," he whispered back.

There was a scuffling sound on the far side of the wall and suddenly the torch reappeared over the top of it, shining down onto their faces.

"Aha!" said a voice behind the torch. "Got you, you little sneaks."

Julia shielded her eyes and blinked up at the torch. She couldn't make out the face behind it, but the voice and the wisps of hair catching the edge of the halo of torchlight were unmistakably Mr Moore's. He had made short work of scaling the boundary wall and surprising them.

Julia decided that the best thing was to go on the attack. In any case there was nowhere to run, so she puffed up her chest and did her best to look defiant while squinting into the glare.

"Did you break into my house today, Mr Moore?" she demanded.

There was a momentary silence from the top of the wall. "What?"

"You heard me. Answer the question."

"No, I didn't break into your house. Since you're here sneaking around my property I rather think *I* should be asking *you* that, don't you?"

"We were just coming to ask you some questions," Mark said.

"At this time of night?" shouted Mr Moore. "I doubt that very much. Now get out of here before I call the police. And I don't want to catch you snooping around my property again."

"Don't worry, you won't," said Mark.

"We'll hide better next time," Julia whispered.

"I heard that," Mr Moore snarled. "Now beat it."

There was a scraping sound as he lowered himself back from the top of the wall into his garden and Julia blinked as her eyes adjusted to the night again.

There was a drawn-out screech and then a clang as the gates closed solidly on them. Julia watched through the bars as Mr Moore stormed back up the driveway towards his home.

She looked despondently to where she knew the cattle grid lay on the other side of the gate.

"My shoe," she said.

Chapter 10

When Mr Peabody – that is Mr Peabody the planning inspectorate and not Mr Peabody the parish treasurer – entered the shop, Julia rather hoped he had come as a customer rather than in his official capacity. He had patronized the shop on occasion before, after all. However, the clipboard held firmly in both hands didn't fill Julia with confidence.

He made his way up to the counter. He had a thin face with a rounded chin, thick glasses and thinning black hair on top. A familiar if not friendly face, he stood before Julia with his bolt-upright bearing and bid her a good morning.

"Good morning, Mr Peabody," Julia returned. "What can I do for you?"

Mr Peabody adjusted his glasses and looked down at his clipboard. "I heard that you have plans to allow another party to buy out the remainder of your lease," he said.

"Well it's not decided yet," Julia said. "They assured me that it was all within the rules though."

"Oh, yes, certainly," Mr Peabody said, with the closest Julia had seen him to expressing emotion. "For all Tammerick Property Services' faults, they do tend to do everything by the book."

Julia swallowed as that sank in. "What faults are those, exactly?"

"It's really not for me to say," Mr Peabody said.

Mr Peabody had a way of being unhelpful, it was never clear to Julia if that was intentional. But either way she doubted if she would wring anything useful out of him. "Well then. If everything is above board with them, what's the reason for you calling today? Are you here to buy a book, Mr Peabody?" she asked, more in hope than expectation.

"Indeed no," Mr Peabody said and gave a reedy laugh although Julia couldn't see the joke herself. "No, I like to get myself ahead of events when I can. I'm just wondering what changes might be required in turning this unit from a bookshop into homes."

With that, Mr Peabody drifted from the counter, making a circuit around the edge of one of the shelves while looking up thoughtfully at the ceiling.

Julia extracted herself from behind the counter and followed him as he went. "What exactly do you mean?" she asked.

"Well, there are so many things to consider. Entry points. Ventilation. Fire risks, although compared to the flammable nature of your merchandise I'm sure domestic units will be fine."

Julia was close on his heels as he arrived at the front window and carefully examined the frames.

"But what do you mean? They want to buy this as a bookshop, don't they?" she asked.

"Yes. Tammerick Property Services wish to buy this as a bookshop," Mr Peabody said, making a quick note on his clipboard before moving on to look at the doorway.

"So they don't want to convert it into homes?"

"They certainly do," said Mr Peabody.

"But you just said…" Julia trailed off, with her finger raised in the air. One of them wasn't making much sense in this conversation. She suspected it was him but wasn't certain.

Mr Peabody gave a long sigh and lowered his clipboard to look directly at Julia. He spoke slowly as though explaining something to a child. "Miss Ford. Tammerick Property Services wish to buy this as a bookshop and then, having bought it, convert it into flats. For commercial reasons, you understand?"

Julia felt the floor spin under her, barely noticing as the planning inspector slid away again to continue his survey. Her mind raced. She was happy to have someone buy the place to continue it as a bookshop. She wasn't so sure she felt the same if they were just going to turn it into flats.

True, it would still neatly get her out of her financial uncertainties, but she wasn't sure if Biddle Rhyne needed poky little flats in the middle of it, compared to something the community could enjoy like her shop. She silenced the little voice in her mind questioning just how much the community were enjoying her shop based on the footfall she saw. Surely only a few loyal customers still meant it was a worthwhile endeavour?

She shook this thought from her mind and hurried to catch up with Mr Peabody who was now in the entry foyer and looking like he was about to make his way back onto the high street.

"But they can't do that, can they?" she asked, her voice just a little louder and more aggressive than she had intended. "Turn this place into flats, I mean."

Mr Peabody turned to face her. "They certainly can."

"Doesn't the planning commission have anything to say?" asked Julia.

"Yes they do," Mr Peabody said.

There was a pause before Julia grunted and carried on. "And what do they say?"

"Well initially there was a lot of resistance," Mr Peabody replied. "But after Tammerick Property Services agreed to build a park as well, they eventually changed their minds."

Julia's mouth swung open a fraction. "Well, they certainly can't be building a park as well," she said.

Mr Peabody raised an eyebrow. "Whyever not, Miss Ford?"

Julia span round indicating the space around them. Admittedly as buildings went it was not exactly tiny. But even two flats, one upstairs and one downstairs, wasn't going to leave acres of room to turn into a children's play area.

"Where are they planning on putting the blooming thing?" she said, feeling the colour rise in her cheeks.

"The park won't be here, obviously," Mr Peabody said.

"Oh." Julia deflated as she said it. Admittedly it made more sense that it might go somewhere else.

"No," Mr Peabody continued, "the park will go along with the other homes."

Apparently considering the conversation over, Mr Peabody turned and walked smartly down the steps onto the pavement. Traffic trundled sedately but steadily down the road next to him.

Dismissing the small chance of a customer arriving, Julia followed him down the high street. "What other homes?" she called after him.

Mr Peabody replied as he continued walking. "Tammerick Property Services have proposed a development that includes the flats here on the high street, as well as six further houses and a play park at the site of the Barley Mow pub," he said.

Mentally Julia tried to envision six more homes crowding in on the space around the Barley Mow and failed. She couldn't think how they would fit them in, although then again she hadn't been able to picture how they would fit four houses onto the site of the old coach house and now there they were, just awaiting the finishing touches.

"Ivan's selling up more land?" Julia asked, hurrying to keep up with Mr Peabody's surprisingly vigorous pace down the road. Poor Ivan, as much as he loved making a profit he must be feeling the pinch if he was willing to surround himself with buildings like that. The pub was his home after all and he'd already lived with the construction work going on around him for some time.

"Ivan Draisaitl is selling the business. Much as you are, Miss Ford," Mr Peabody said.

"No, that can't be right, Ivan would never do that," Julia said.

Ivan pretty much was the Barley Mow. He'd poured his heart and soul into keeping the place running. Not only running but thriving. Julia had a wealth of memories contained within the whitewashed walls of that place, and she was sure half the village did too.

"Mr Draisaitl has already agreed terms with Tammerick Property Services, Miss Ford," Mr Peabody said, stopping smartly at a sideroad as a bicycle rushed past before continuing. "I believe it is, as they say, a done deal. The planning commission has already given it their approval. It is only formalities to be decided now. Although it is contingent on the sale of your shop as well."

"It is? Why?" said Julia, dodging a surprisingly quiet second cyclist and taking a long step over a lingering puddle onto the far pavement.

"The development needs to meet its quota of affordable housing," Mr Peabody said.

Julia did her best to digest this, not fully realizing that she was still following along quietly at Mr Peabody's heels.

When he reached the turn-off for the council offices he gave Julia a glance over his shoulder.

"Miss Ford, don't you have a shop to mind?"

"Oh," Julia said, stopping in her tracks. For now she did. "Yes. Yes I do."

"Well in that case I will say farewell," Mr Peabody said, disappearing up the road towards his offices.

Julia turned around and walked hurriedly back the way she had come. She couldn't believe that Ivan would be shutting the pub. The thought had just never occurred to her. The village wouldn't be the same without it. It would still have the Fox and Hounds, but that just didn't compare. It lacked all the charm and atmosphere of the Barley Mow.

She shook her head as she pushed through the entrance foyer and back into the shop. Unsurprisingly it was completely empty. A shop with no customers didn't really need a shopkeeper.

She sat heavily down on the stool behind the counter. Was it really worth keeping this place running? Perhaps it would be better as flats. People needed somewhere to live after all.

She glanced down at the time on her phone. As soon as she was done here she was going to talk to Ivan. Perhaps Mr Peabody had been wrong after all.

* * *

When Julia let herself into the parlour of the Barley Mow it was empty, save for Ivan behind the bar, looking sullen even though he was framed by the colourful bunting for the fête. As she made her way over to him, Julia caught the sounds of a couple of voices drifting through from the dining room next door. It seemed Ivan wasn't entirely on his own, then.

Never idle, the landlord had a biro in hand and was looking over the staff rota as Julia approached. Normally he would have quickly hidden it away and paid attention when a customer arrived. But as ex-staff herself, it seemed Julia didn't quite count and all she got was an uninterested grunt when she arrived and his eyes hardly looked up.

"Hi, Ivan," Julia said to the hair on the top of his head which was currently being presented to her.

"Hi, Julia," Ivan muttered, striking a line through one of the names and penning something else in its place.

Finally he looked up at her and gave a half-hearted smile, more because form demanded it, Julia thought, than through any real feeling.

"If you're looking for your friend then you just missed him," Ivan said. "He left about five minutes ago."

"My friend?" Julia looked puzzled. "Which friend?"

Ivan waved a large hand over to the table which sat beside the hearth. "The young chap you were in here with the other day."

It took Julia a second to realize who he meant: Beatrice's nephew, Tony.

"Oh, he's not a friend. He's related to a case I'm looking into," Julia said.

Whatever was he doing in the Barley Mow though? It's a free country, but when they met here before, Tony said he'd had trouble finding the place, so it evidently wasn't a regular haunt of his. As much as Ivan ran a nice pub, she wasn't sure it would draw someone straight back like that.

"Was he here with anyone?" Julia asked.

"No, just him. He had half a lemonade and then left," Ivan said.

Even more puzzling. Julia hovered at the bar for a moment considering going after him. But even if she knew what direction he'd gone in, after five minutes there was little chance of catching him up. And even if she did, what would she do? Demand that he justify why he'd been in the Barley Mow?

"So if you weren't meeting this man, what brings you into my fine establishment?" Ivan said.

Julia smiled at him. "Can't I just drop in for a drink?" she asked.

"Based on recent trends, no," Ivan said. "At least unless Sally is behind the bar and capable of slipping you free refills when she thinks I'm not looking."

Julia blushed. "Actually I came to talk to you, Ivan."

"To me? What about?"

"Mr Peabody was in the shop today."

Ivan gave an unimpressed squint. "And what did he want?"

Julia had forgotten that the landlord had had run-ins with Mr Peabody before over the houses built on the site of the old coach house.

"He didn't really want much of anything," Julia said, "but he told me that you had agreed to sell the Barley Mow."

"Hm. Well, that's right," Ivan said.

It was hard to tell how he was feeling about it. Perhaps he didn't know himself.

"I didn't believe it until I heard it from you," Julia said. "It's hard to imagine Biddle Rhyne without this place. And without you."

Finally Ivan's face softened slightly. "Yeah, well," he said, wiping distractedly at something on the bar. "It's not as easy making ends meet these days. Wages are up. Heating is up. Food prices are up. But raise my prices and everyone will just eat in the cheap places in King's Barrow instead. You know how it is."

Julia thought back to her largely empty shop. "Yes, I suppose I do," she said.

"Still, it will give me a chance to try my hand at something new, won't it?" Ivan said, his cheerfulness just a little forced.

Julia didn't know what she might do without the shop; she had thought she'd be angling for work at the Barley Mow if she'd sold it. "And what will you try your hand at?" Julia asked.

Ivan laughed. "It's a good question, I'm no spring chicken. Maybe I'll find a rich, beautiful woman and become a kept man. I think that would suit me."

Julia couldn't imagine Ivan being very good at doing nothing, she was so used to seeing him buzzing about, always busy at something.

She felt a cold breeze on her back and turned to see a group of customers coming in, chattering to themselves as they ducked under the low oak beams and made for the bar.

"Well, I'll get out of your hair," Julia said. "If that man's in here again though, the one from my case, can you let me know?"

"Sure," Ivan said, and turned a broad smile to the approaching group. As he did so, he slid the staff rota away out of sight under the bar.

Julia edged away to make room at the bar and headed for home.

* * *

As soon as Julia was through the front door, Sally's voice called to her from the kitchen. "Come here, Julia, I've found something really odd!"

Julia hurried in, pulling her coat off as she went. "What is it?"

Sally was standing at the kitchen counter. In front of her were two open Tupperware boxes, each containing an ice cream cake.

"My cake has multiplied," Sally observed wryly. "I only left one in the freezer and now there are two."

Julia gave a fleeting glance down at the two cakes as she made her way to the kettle and filled it. "The amount you've been baking I'm sure you must have made two and forgotten about one," she said.

"Hardly likely," Sally said. She gave the rightmost cake a prod with one of her long nails. "And look, this one is all wonky and misshapen. Whatever could have gone wrong with it?"

That did it. Julia span around to face her friend, her pitch rising with the whine of the kettle. "There's nothing wrong with it!"

Sally declined to reply, but with deliberate movements she replaced the lids on the two Tupperwares and put them both back into the freezer. Julia felt hers was dropped in rather roughly. If it was misshapen then it was probably because Sally had battered it around.

Silence settled on the kitchen as the kettle reached its boil and then clicked off. Julia pushed her tea bag around the cup a few times as she waited for it to brew. Sally stood with her arms folded across her chest, watching.

Finally, as Julia was leaving with her tea, Sally spoke. "How is your Hurricane chocolate cake coming along, chicken?" she asked.

"Just fine, I'm sure I'll perfect it in time for the bake-off," Julia said, and swept upstairs to her room.

Chapter 11

Julia found herself unable to settle that evening. Sally had commandeered the kitchen again, and Julia felt in no mood to share. And obviously surveilling Mr Moore in person again was out of the question, after the last time.

Her phone chimed softly with a message, and she snatched it up. It was only junk email, but an idea was forming in her mind.

She had always considered herself fairly accomplished at stalking people on social media. In the past that had generally been men she was interested in or women who she thought were interested in the men she was interested in.

It felt strange to be using her powers for good.

It took her a short while to get going in earnest. She had changed the passwords for all of her online accounts after the break-in and now she kept forgetting half of them.

But eventually she had everything up and running and was plugging Mr Moore's name into various social media sites to see what fell out.

She was still at it when Mark let himself in, giving her a greeting which went unreturned.

"Here, look at this," Julia said, eyes fixed on her phone.

"Hello to you too," he said, but looked at Julia's phone screen all the same.

"It looks like Mr Moore was at some graphic design event the night Beatrice was killed," Julia said.

She pointed to the column of photos on her screen.

Mr Moore looked entirely different with his hair combed back and a smartly ironed shirt on. He was also smiling which changed his features rather dramatically. Still, he was almost a head taller than most of the people he was standing next to in the photos. A banner visible in the background of some of them read 'The Future of Photoshop'.

"So he has an alibi then," said Mark.

"Perhaps," Julia said. She began scrolling back up the photos. "Look at this. In some of the photos it's daylight outside. But not any that Mr Moore appears in. I reckon it must be dark outside by the time he arrived."

"He likes to be fashionably late," Mark said mirthlessly.

"Or he had somewhere else he needed to be," Julia said.

"Like Beatrice's flat," Mark finished for her, and sank down into the sofa.

Rumpkin came padding over and climbed up next to Mark.

As Mark patted the dog idly, he said, "So how do we find out where he was earlier in the night? I get the impression he's not just going to tell us if we ask him."

"He might tell Freiland though," Julia said.

Mark scoffed. "We can try but I don't think she'll do us any favours."

"Or your dad," Julia said.

"Possibly," Mark said. "But all the same, all Mr Moore needs to do is claim he left a little late for his work do."

Julia thought for a moment. "If we can find his car number plate then maybe your dad can track where he's been."

Mark sat up, ignoring Rumpkin's whine for attention. "Yeah, maybe," he said. "See if he was anywhere near Beatrice's."

"Exactly," Julia said.

"Give my dad a call then," Mark said.

* * *

Julia spent all of the next day waiting for Jones to call her back. When the phone finally did ring she pounced on it and snatched it up, but it was the Barley Mow calling. She recognized the number easily enough, it was imprinted on her mind from her days working there. When she answered the call it was Sally's voice she heard.

"Hi, Julia," Sally said. "Ivan asked me to call you. That lad's back in the pub again. Tony."

Julia sat up and began hunting for her keys. Mark gave her a questioning look which she ignored for the time being.

"What's he doing?" Julia asked.

"Nothing much," said Sally. "Just sat at a table in the corner by himself."

It was definitely odd that he'd settled on the Barley Mow as his regular pub now.

"I'll be right there," Julia said. "If he leaves, can you call me?"

"Sure. My shift's finishing soon though."

"Sally…" Julia pleaded.

"Fine, but be quick."

"I will." Julia hung up and began pulling on her shoes.

"What's up?" Mark asked her.

Julia quickly explained what was going on.

"I'll come too," Mark said. "In case he's dangerous."

Julia couldn't see Tony being much of a threat, especially inside the pub, but the lift was appreciated anyway and she didn't want him disappearing again before she arrived, so she didn't argue.

Soon they were pulling off the lane, over the long, shallow puddle and onto the gravel expanse of the Barley Mow's car park. Julia made a quick note of the other cars, since one of them would be Tony's.

A fine drizzle had started falling, and Julia hurried over to the parlour door as much because of the rain as to make sure she caught Tony.

As she stepped inside, she saw Tony at one of the tables on the side of the room under the window. A mostly empty pint of lemonade sat fizzing away before him and he had his phone out in front of him, although he seemed to be looking over the top of it. Their eyes locked as soon as Julia was in the room.

She realized that despite her eagerness to get here and see what was what, she didn't have any plan. She forced herself to smile and made her way over to Tony, hoping her acting skills were up to snuff.

"Oh, hi!" she said, trying to sound surprised. "Fancy running into you here. What are you up to?"

Tony lowered his phone. His hair had been styled, compared to when they had met before, and she could smell the scent of his aftershave over the top of the usual background smells of the pub: old oak, old fires, and old beer.

"I'm just, you know, hanging out," he said quietly. Julia thought she could detect a slight blush.

Mark put an arm on Julia's shoulder and leaned around her to address them both. "I'll get some drinks in. Julia, wine? How about you, can I get you something?" he said to Tony.

Tony looked up at Mark and swallowed then shook his head. "I'm all right, thank you," he said.

"If you're sure." Mark slid his arm off and headed up to the quiet bar, greeting Sally from halfway across the room. Tony's eyes followed him as he went.

"Do you mind if I join you?" Julia asked, indicating a chair and settling down into it. She had a view of both Tony and the rest of the room from there.

Failing to think of anything more to say that would prise information out of the young man, Julia sat in awkward silence watching Mark at the bar. He exchanged a few words with Sally in a low voice as she poured and then he made his way back to the table.

Just as he seated himself the parlour door opened again and Charlie came in, apparently not spotting them and making straight for the bar. He leaned his tall frame over it, giving Sally a peck on the cheek before straightening up.

Sally called over her shoulder to the back of the pub. "Ivan! I'm going now!"

A reply came rumbling back, completely inaudible to Julia and presumably to Sally as well. But that didn't stop her lifting up the bar flap and linking arms with Charlie as they headed out the door. She gave Julia's table a little wave as they went.

"Goodbye," Julia called after her.

Tony lifted his glass to his lips and quickly finished the rest of his drink, stifling a burp at the end of it. Julia couldn't help thinking he looked slightly crestfallen.

"Nice to see you again, I need to be going," he mumbled, sliding from his chair and grabbing a jumper from the back of it.

"Goodbye, Tony," Julia said, but he was already halfway out of the door.

"Very strange," she said to Mark.

Mark took a sip from his bottle of beer. "Not that strange," he said. He lifted the bottle up and inspected the label. "Say, can you charge Ronald expenses for these?"

Julia ignored that. "What do you mean it's not strange? What's he up to then?"

Mark gave a broad grin. "I would say that he has a little crush on someone," he said.

Julia raised her eyebrows. "No, I don't think he has a crush on me. Does he?"

Mark laughed gently. "Not on you," he said.

"Oh."

* * *

Julia's phone rang just as she was leaving the pub and she hurried to dig through her bag and retrieve it. This time it was Jones calling.

"Hello, Rhys," she said.

"Hi, Julia," he said. "I've run Brad Moore's plates through the system for you."

"And?" Julia asked expectantly.

Mark leaned his ear in towards the phone, trying to listen in.

"A camera did pick his car up a couple of streets away from Beatrice Campbell's place around the time of her murder," Jones said.

Julia tried and failed to suppress a squeal of vindication, making Mark jump. "I knew it!"

"All right, don't get too excited," Jones said to her. "It doesn't prove anything much. It's a main road and what's more, it's a main road between his house and this Photoshop thingy you said he was at. He could well have been on his way there."

"But he arrived there late," Julia said.

"Being late isn't a crime," said Jones.

"It depends on what makes you late," Julia replied.

She heard Jones groan. "Like I said, it doesn't prove anything."

"Is it enough for you to pick him up?" Julia asked.

"Firstly, no it isn't. Secondly, it would be Freiland who would pick him up, or not, remember?"

Julia scowled at the phone. Freiland was fixated on Ronald Cutty. There was no way she was going to grill Brad Moore. She had hoped Jones would have done her a bit more of a favour. "And what about the fingerprints?" she asked him. "The ones from the break-in."

"Okay, well I did find a set of prints that didn't match anyone from the house. They were on the window and on your laptop," said Jones.

Julia gave a satisfied 'hmph' sound, which she hoped didn't lose its meaning over the phone line.

"However, it didn't match anything on the databases so you're looking at someone who doesn't currently have a criminal record," said Jones.

"And does Mr Moore have a criminal record?" Julia asked.

There was a brief pause before the policeman replied. "No, he doesn't."

"Thanks, Rhys," she said.

"Take care, Julia," he replied. "I mean that."

Julia thought for a moment. "We're going to have to find a way to get to Mr Moore again," she said.

Mark made a non-committal noise and carried on across the car park.

Julia trailed after him but she wasn't really paying attention. This time she had to make sure they didn't get spotted. Or lose any more footwear. It might take some planning. But in the meantime there was baking that needed to be done; the fête was tomorrow.

Chapter 12

Julia stood on the bottom step of the bookshop entrance waiting for the parade to start. The pavements weren't exactly thronged, but there was a broken line of people on each side of the road. Admittedly most of them were parents of the schoolchildren who would make up the bulk of the parade.

Scanning up and down the high street, a few of the shops and other businesses had strung up bunting or little flags. Julia wondered briefly if she should have done so as well, but she couldn't honestly say that she was that enthused by the occasion and it would have been more than a little cynical to do so just to try and drum up business.

Besides, it couldn't really have drummed up many more sales, could it? There had been a small bump in her customers today from the extra footfall, a few colourful bits of fabric weren't likely to send them into the shop in droves.

Looking up and down the street again in order to make a mental tally of the premises with flags against those without, Julia spotted a face she knew in the crowd.

Dillon was just up the road, doing his best to get through the knots of people. He looked rather determined in his walk. He seemed to have a purpose and Julia had no doubt that purpose was finding her. It certainly seemed rather unlikely he was here just to soak in the festival atmosphere.

Julia quickly ducked back into the shop and pressed her back against the door. What should she do? He must surely have found out by now that she and Mark weren't with the police as she had let him believe. She kicked herself. Why had she done that? Of course he would find out, and even if he hadn't been moved to come and seek her out, the chances were that she would need to visit Ronald's offices at some point soon. As usual, she'd gone about making trouble for herself.

Hopefully Dillon hadn't seen her yet. He was still a good way up the street, Julia had only spotted him because he stood a head above most of the other people in the crowd.

Moving quickly, Julia flicked the sign on the door to 'closed' and dashed from the entrance foyer into the main shop, flicking the lights off as she went.

She wasn't a moment too soon because two seconds later she heard the gentle click of someone trying the door into the foyer.

As ever, it was dim inside the shop, and the shelves provided a pretty effective screen from the window. But all the same, Julia flung herself down behind the counter for good measure.

There came a pounding on the front door and she heard Dillon's voice calling out her name.

She found herself holding her breath as she crouched. She knew it was stupid. She was still going to have to face Dillon when she next went to Ronald's firm. But at least at the offices there would be enough people around to prevent Dillon from throttling her. Ronald would intervene on her behalf, wouldn't he?

She stayed quiet as there was one more knock and after that no more followed.

She risked peeking out round the side of the counter and was rewarded with seeing Dillon's figure trailing away down the street. She let out a deep breath, stood up and dusted off her knees.

"I really need to sweep that floor more often," she muttered.

Taking one more peek out of the window to satisfy herself that Dillon had given up, Julia turned the lights back on and flipped the sign round again to 'open'.

Up the road, the raggedy procession lurched into motion and the children were soon trooping past the shop. Leaning forward against the glass to look, Julia could see them turn off a little way down the road, heading for the village green. It would seem that Ivan hadn't been able to entice the local council to finish at the Barley Mow after all.

The three dozen or so children of Biddle Rhyne's primary school had dressed up for the occasion. One or two were in completely unidentifiable outfits of cardboard and crepe paper, but the predominant theme was World War II get-ups, with Hurricane pilots being the most numerous. One poor child was dressed as the Hurricane itself, cardboard wings stretching almost the whole width of the street as the child veered this way and that trying to keep their balance as they hurried along behind their faster and less encumbered classmates.

The bell rang and a moment later Mark appeared next to her. He was looking relatively smart, for him, which meant not covered in paint. He'd agreed to mind the shop for the final hour or so, so that Julia could present her efforts at the bake-off.

"All ready to go?" he asked.

Julia watched the cardboard Hurricane stumble, perhaps in an effort to re-enact the fabled crash, and scramble back up and hurry out of sight round the bend.

"I'm ready, I'll just go and grab my cakes," Julia said, giving Mark a quick kiss and heading to the back room.

With an oversized Tupperware hooked under one arm and handbag hanging off the other, Julia joined the stream of parents following after the children's parade, turning off the high street and towards the village green.

Biddle Rhyne's green was not huge, and today it felt positively packed. Stalls of various descriptions lined two sides, selling local produce. Competing honeys and jams were well represented. At the far end a hog roast was being turned, the smell of the cooking meat had been tantalizing Julia whenever the wind had blown towards the shop.

The children swarmed the middle of the green, running about with no discernible order to them over the short grass and the daisies. The weather had been kind, with a clear blue sky overhead and the sun shining down. In fact, the air was feeling positively hot now. Various layers of costume had been stripped off and discarded in an effort to keep cool. Harried-looking parents were picking over the field looking for the items which belonged to their child.

At the far end of the green, the pale grey stone of the church tower rose, almost glowing in the sunlight. The ancient, square prominence had been scrubbed clean recently, to the vicar's delight.

On the final side of the green from the village, the low wooden building of the village hall nestled among a line of trees. Next to the double doors of the entrance, a white flagpole rose up and the Union Jack flapped and snapped in the breeze.

The duck pond lay just beside it, the site of Major Portland's infamous motoring mishap. Although the frenzy of youngsters running up and down the bank of the pond and making enthusiastic but ill-judged attempts to skim stones meant that the ducks had fled hours earlier.

The air was filled with the sound of laughter, the occasional excited bark of a dog and the smell of cooking food. People were milling about, chatting and enjoying the day. Children were running around, playing games and chasing each other. The atmosphere was relaxed and jovial.

Only as Julia approached the village hall did the atmosphere start to take on more of an edge.

Trestle tables had been set out in front of the entrance of the hall in a long line, with triangular bunting strung along the underside of them to brighten them up. Mismatched tablecloths covered the tops and Biddle Rhyne's baking hopefuls were rushing to and fro with frenetic energy, laying out plates and cake dishes. They jostled one another for whatever they considered prime position on the tables ahead of the judging, which Julia had been told would be at 5 p.m. sharp.

As Julia reached the tables she saw Mr Smedley, the garden centre manager, assembling a three-tier cake stand of white china with gold gilt edges and a floral design painted on. Watching him, it dawned on her that she had only her Tupperware box to present her offering. At this rate she could only be hoping for a sympathy prize.

And there next to him was Mrs Burns. Whatever she had baked was hidden underneath a tea towel. As was the top half of the woman, as she fiddled with whatever needing fiddling with. Julia recognized Mrs Burns only from her bottom which was protruding from under the towel. Why there was a need for such secrecy this late in proceedings, Julia couldn't say. She squeezed her way past Mrs Burns's rear end and down the table to Sally. On the tablecloth in front of her a couple of the best plates from home were laid out – Julia's own plates she noted – but they were currently bare, except for a couple of intrepid flies which Sally kept shooing away by flicking her fingers. It seemed it wasn't only Mrs Burns who was keeping her cards close to her chest.

"You're not keeping yours a secret still, are you?" Julia asked. "Who can copy you now?" She might expect this behaviour from Mrs Burns but really it was beneath Sally.

"No," Sally said, blowing sharply on one of the plates to dislodge a particularly persistent fly. She indicated over her shoulder to the village hall. "They're keeping cool in the freezer there. It's too early for them to come out."

Julia looked in the direction Sally had indicated. The doors of the village hall were open but there was a chair placed in front of them with a sign on it saying 'Fête Staff Only'. It was, of course, just like Sally to sweet-talk her way into getting some extra privileges.

A shadow fell over the table and as Julia looked up her heart dropped. Mr Tinkler loomed over them, a scornful look on his face, which was still bearing a faint suntan from his jaunt to Spain.

"Why if it isn't our meddlesome little private detective," he sneered.

Julia didn't know how to respond to that and muttered a hello back under her breath, hugging her Tupperware close to her chest for protection.

Mr Tinkler peered down at the box. "I hope your baking is better than your detective work," he said. "Not that it's a high bar to stumble over with this lot."

"Hey," Sally said, eyes aflame.

"You seem to have forgotten yours, love," Mr Tinkler said, looking briefly at Sally's empty plates.

He looked theatrically up and down the trestle tables at the cakes arrayed along them. "It's a pathetic lot really though, isn't it?"

"What's your problem?" said Sally.

"Oh, no problem," said Mr Tinkler. "Quite the opposite. The one silver lining of not being able to afford to sponsor this dog and pony show this year is that I don't have to pretend to like it."

Sally opened her mouth for a rebuttal but he turned his back on her before she could reply. "Now, if you girls will excuse me, I think I'm going to go and find something more engaging to do. Stick my head in the duck pond perhaps."

With that, Mr Tinkler set off with his stiff gaited walk into the crowd.

"Who on earth is he?" Sally said.

"Oh" – Julia sighed and placed her Tupperware down next to Sally's plates and unclipped the lid – "that's Finn Tinkler. One of the embezzlement victims."

"It couldn't have happened to a nicer person," Sally remarked.

"True. No one seems to like him," Julia said, rearranging her cakes in a half-hearted attempt to make them look more appealing."

"Well, someone likes him," Sally said archly.

"What do you mean?" Julia asked.

But before Sally could answer they were interrupted by the reverend clapping his hands together loudly at the end of the tables.

"Fifteen minutes, bakers," the vicar called, his high-pitched voice cutting across the chatter. "Fifteen minutes until the judging."

"I'd better get my cake out of the freezer," Sally said, and hurried past the chair and into the shadows of the village hall.

Julia looked down at her own cakes and began transferring them onto one of the plates Sally had brought. She did have two and they were, after all, Julia's plates.

She had just finished placing the last one down when an awful scream came from the village hall.

Julia spun, feeling the colour drain from her face. That had been Sally's scream, she knew it.

As other faces turned to look at the hall in puzzlement, Julia sprang into action, dashing past the chair and bounding into the hall.

It was dark inside, a stark contrast to the golden sunshine out on the green, and Julia had to stop just inside the hall as her eyes adjusted.

The hall itself was empty, but the side door at the far end was open and Julia ran across the creaking floorboards, her handbag swinging as she went.

She burst through the door and into the kitchen.

Sally looked up as the door banged open, colliding with the wall and taking a chunk of plaster out as it did so. She had a look of stunned disbelief on her face.

"Look," Sally managed, raising a trembling finger to point.

One of Julia's plates sat on the forma counter next to the fridge freezer. It was covered in a gloopy mess which Julia could just identify as cake.

The jumble of red and blue squares made it still identifiable as Sally's signature Britainberg. But they were soggy and limp, the ice cream that bound them together now just a sticky white puddle that filled the shallow plate and was dripping off onto the counter beneath.

A tear ran down Sally's cheek. "Someone took it out of the freezer," she said.

Julia put her arm around her friend and guided her slowly back into the main hall so she wouldn't be subjected to looking at it anymore.

"There there, it's okay," Julia said.

"No it's not, it's completely ruined," said Sally.

The vicar and a few of the bakers were cautiously making their way into the hall to see what was causing the commotion and if they could help, or at the very least observe.

"What's the matter?" the vicar asked, seeing the two distressed women approaching.

"Someone took Sally's ice cream cake out of the freezer," Julia said.

"It's sabotage," Sally said.

"Pfft," a dismissive noise came from Mrs Burns. "I expect the girl just forgot to put the cake in," she said, raising her voice and addressing the room at large.

"Do you think I'm an idiot?" Sally barked back.

"Well–" Mrs Burns began.

Luckily a thought struck Julia and she held Sally by the shoulders, turning her to face her. "I think I can rescue this," she whispered.

Sally shook her head, tears still welling up. She wiped them away with the back of her wrist. "How?"

"Just trust me," Julia said, glancing up at the clock on the wall. She turned to the vicar. "Reverend, can we hold off judging?"

Mrs Burns answered on his behalf. "Rules are rules, I'm afraid, Miss Ford. Something your generation should probably learn."

The vicar held his hands out in a helpless gesture. "It might not be fair to the other contestants," he said.

Hovering at his shoulder, Mrs Burns beamed.

"I suppose I could put off judging Sally's cake until last though, if it helps," the vicar suggested.

"It will have to do," Julia said. She made a large sweeping gesture at the crowd in front of her. "Out of the way please, out of the way!"

The crowd shuffled slowly apart to form an aisle and Julia ran as fast as she could towards the door of the hall.

As she hurried out of the hall she banged into the chair and it toppled onto the grass. Recovering her stride, she shot a glance up at the clock on the church tower and swore under her breath. She altered course heading straight for the line of bushes behind the hog roast which separated the village green from the streets behind. She was going to have to take a shortcut that she hadn't taken for a very long time indeed.

* * *

The church bells were just chiming quarter to the hour when Julia re-emerged through the gap in the hedge, which had seemed much wider when she was a teenager, and came panting and wheezing back onto the village green. She asked herself, not for the first time in recent months, why she didn't keep up with any cardio practice.

Held in front of her was another Tupperware box, and she did her best to minimize the amount of jostling as she ran. Although given the pace which she currently had been reduced to, the box remained fairly steady in her hands.

Through the milling crowds scattered over the green, Julia could see the vicar making his way along the tables. She saw him lifting a small morsel of something from one of the cake stands. He was still judging then, so she wasn't too late.

Julia redoubled her efforts, hopping over the cardboard Hurricane wings which now lay discarded, and closing the distance to the bakers.

Sally looked round as she heard Julia approaching. Her face was tear-stained and her make-up was smudged. But she managed a smile.

"I don't understand. What's in there?" Sally asked as Julia arrived breathless beside her and placed the Tupperware down gently on the tablecloth.

Julia was too out of breath to reply so she flicked the clips on the lid instead and lifted it off.

Sally looked inside. "But I can't present your cake," she said.

Julia reached in and carefully selected one of the slices from the middle, lifting the chilled cake from the box and placing it with as much ceremony as she could onto the plate.

"Make sure the vicar eats this one, it's yours," Julia said, finally recovering enough to talk. "The others can just be garnish."

Sally peered in close and inspected the slice of cake with an expert eye. "That *is* one of mine, isn't it?" she said. "But I still don't understand."

Julia couldn't meet her friend's eye. "I pilfered it," she said quietly. "For research. I'm sorry."

Sally's face melted. "Don't be sorry," she said and wrapped Julia up in a hug. "You've saved my bake-off."

Julia hugged Sally back and then looked up to see where the vicar had got to. It seemed that he only had Mrs Burns left to judge before he reached them.

Mrs Burns stood to attention by her bake. As the vicar sidled across to her she whipped the tea towel away with a flourish.

Julia and Sally gasped in unison. Sitting on the plate Mrs Burns had revealed was undoubtedly an ice cream cake. She must have been fiddling with a coolbox underneath the towel earlier because now the cake was beautifully laid out with a slice cut ready to eat.

What's more, the slice was the crisply chequered blue and red, with pristine white ice cream forming a Union Jack pattern.

"That's my Britainberg," Sally hissed to Julia.

Julia gaped. Sally was right.

"How did she know?" Sally said. "Did you…?"

"No!" Julia whispered back. "Of course I didn't."

"She must have been spying on us," said Sally.

The vicar looked suitably impressed at the cake before him. "Very lovely presentation, Mrs Burns," he trilled.

"Why thank you, Vicar," she peeped back.

The vicar slowly extended his hand and picked the slice up between thumb and forefinger. He took a small bite and chewed on it thoughtfully.

"Is that a hint of matcha, I detect?" he asked.

The vicar did have a good palette. He hadn't only been selected to be the bake-off judge because of his high standing in the community.

Sally was shaking with rage now. "Matcha tea? That was my secret ingredient," she hissed.

Julia was gobsmacked. So that was the missing element that she had failed to reproduce. How on earth had Mrs Burns found that out when even she couldn't?

Her friend nudged her sharply in the ribs with her elbow. "That break-in…" Sally said.

"No!" Julia couldn't bring herself to believe it.

"She did," said Sally. "That cow. She broke in just to get a look at my recipe."

"Well, I can guess who took your cake out of the freezer too," Julia said, watching the vicar as he dabbed his lips with a napkin and moved on.

Julia and Sally both forced smiles to their lips as the vicar approached in front of them.

He rubbed his hands together. "So, what do we have here?" he said, looking down at Julia's cakes.

"These are chocolate Hurricane cakes with buttercream frosting," Julia said, managing somehow to sound pleasant as the vicar inspected them.

"And they're Hurricane cakes because…" the vicar prompted.

"Because of the swirls on top," Julia said quietly, making a circular motion in the air above them with one of her fingers.

He plucked one up and with only a little difficulty was able to extract it from its casing. He took a small bite from the top of it. "Mmm, that's most tasty," the vicar said, but even Julia could tell that he didn't truly mean it.

The vicar moved quickly on to Sally's cake.

He paused as he looked down at it. "I see it's another ice cream Union Jack," he said finally.

"A Britainberg," she mumbled. Poor Sally, it should have been her moment of triumph after all her hard work.

The vicar's eyes flickered up from the cake to look at her. Did he suspect what had gone on? Julia thought he probably did, but he wasn't about to throw aspersions about.

He said in a quiet voice, "I'm afraid I'll just have to try some and give an honest assessment on which is better," he said.

Sally gave a little nod. "I understand, Vicar," she said.

The vicar's hand descended.

"Um, not that slice, Vicar," Julia said, deep down acutely aware of her own baking abilities. "It got a bit battered around getting it here. That one there survived the best, I think."

The vicar picked up the indicated slice and lifted it up from amongst the cuckoos in the nest. He gave the slice a nibble and chewed with a thoughtful expression on his face.

"Well," he said. "I think I have a verdict."

* * *

The bakers gathered at the head of the trestle tables, forming a little huddle. The vicar was at the centre of it, going through some lengthy preambles before he announced the competition's winner.

The fête was beginning to wind down now. The sun was lowering in the sky and the day had cooled to a more pleasant temperature. The church tower cast a long finger of shadow which stretched across the village green. The grass was patchy in places after a day of hard use. But spring was in full flow now and it would be growing back quickly enough.

A hand laid on Julia's shoulder made her jump and she turned to see Mark smiling down at her.

"How's everything going?" he asked, keeping his voice low so as not to interrupt the vicar, although it would probably have taken more than that to derail him once he was in his stride. "You're looking a little flushed."

Julia blew at a strand of hair which had become loose in the day's activities. She was sticky and sweaty from all of her gadding about in the sunshine and she was fairly sure that it showed. She must be in such a state.

"I'm shattered," Julia said, leaning against Mark for support.

"I didn't know baking was such an exertion," he said.

"Neither did I," Julia replied.

Mark frowned slightly and put an arm around Julia. "Who won?" he asked.

"We're getting to that," Julia said.

The vicar smiled at the small crowd. "Which brings me to the happy task of announcing our winner." There was a general shuffling in front of him as he paused for dramatic effect.

"Sally Hughes," the vicar pronounced.

There was a smattering of applause from the bakers around them. Julia would have liked to have said she was the most enthusiastic among them, but in all honesty her energy was rapidly deserting her and it was all she could manage to join the half-hearted clapping and murmur 'well done' to her. Luckily Mark took up the duty, bringing his hands together and calling out raucously.

Mrs Burns on the other hand made a disapproving clicking noise and, with a haughty expression, she turned and marched down the trestle tables where she began to loudly collect her plates together.

Sally blushed slightly as she went up to the vicar to accept her prize, although it didn't stop an ear-to-ear grin splitting her face. Normally Mr Tinkler's patronage of the competition meant that the vouchers were quite generous. The last-minute nature of his withdrawal meant all Sally gained was a £15 voucher for the garden centre, but she still seemed quite pleased as the vicar handed it to her.

"And although I'm not a sporting man myself, I understand that in most competitions the wooden spoon is something to be dreaded," said the vicar. He picked up just such an item from the table in front of him, engraved with the words 'Biddle Rhyne Bake Off Champion'. "But happily, here no such rule applies. Congratulations, Sally."

Sally posed briefly with the vicar while a photograph was taken and then returned to Mark and Julia clutching her voucher and the spoon.

"Good work, Sally," Julia said.

She smiled at her friend. "Thank you. You know, for everything."

"What's gone on here?" Mark asked, looking from one to the other as they exchanged a knowing glance.

Julia did her best to tame her escaping hair. "That's a long story," she said. "You know what, how about I tell you over a drink? I think I feel like a glass of wine."

Mark reached out and squeezed Julia gently just above her hip. "No you don't," he said.

Chapter 13

The Fox and Hounds was situated on Biddle Rhyne's high street. It was a tall, stone building fronting straight onto the pavement. The rather grand entrance, with gold lettering over the doorway, concealed the slightly rough, grubby interior of the place. The hanging baskets either side of the door, long devoid of any life, gave some hint, however.

Today, it was packed inside. People had evidently been drifting in throughout the day to escape the heat, the crowds, or simply their families. Many of those who had not made it in time had been broiled as bright red as lobsters in the unseasonable sunshine.

But despite the press of bodies it was still much cooler inside than outside. The thick stone walls and relative paucity of windows saw to that. The three of them made their way over the thinly carpeted floor, which was always sticky but today more so than usual. It would seem that it had been recently refreshed with spilt lager and cider.

It was actually where Julia and Mark had first met. Although luckily their relationship had blossomed despite its inauspicious start.

Julia kept a lookout for a free table as they shuffled in stages closer to the bar, but to no avail.

Eventually they reached the front of the queue. A looping string of Union Jacks had been tacked over the bar, dangling down just above eye level.

"What do you think?" Sally asked her, as she tried to catch the eye of a staff member behind the bar. "A whole bottle?"

Julia thought back over the afternoon. "That's probably best," she said.

Eventually Mark managed to get their order in. While the barmaid was pouring his pint, Julia peered at her between the low-hanging flags.

"It's nice to see you get in the spirit of the fête," Julia said. "I guess it brings you a lot of business." She felt a little guilty that despite working just down the road she rarely set foot in here. Her loyalties lay with the Barley Mow, she supposed. Although the Fox and Hounds had geographic convenience in its favour, that didn't outweigh its less seemly qualities.

The barmaid placed the drink down on the bar. "It does," she said. "And the owner's always keen to get into the fête. Did you know that when they set off to rescue that crashed plane, this was where they set off from?"

Julia smiled politely. "I did not know that," she said.

As Julia picked her drink off the bar she felt a sharp elbow in the ribcage.

"Free table," Sally hissed, and before the words were even out of her mouth she was off through the bar in a strange serpentining route through the throngs.

By the time Julia caught up with her, Sally was already happily perched on one of the seats, the discarded glasses cleared to the far end. Julia and Mark climbed up to join her.

"Tell me about this bake-off then," Mark said. "It was eventful, was it?"

"That's an understatement," said Julia.

She opened her mouth to tell him more but then she froze, jaw hanging open and eyes staring across the crowded pub.

"What is it?" Mark asked, turning to follow her eyeline.

"Don't look," Julia said, grabbing Mark's stubbly chin between thumb and forefinger and swivelling it towards the bare wall behind her.

"Why not?" Mark managed, the words garbled.

Julia released the vice-like grip on him, trusting him not to move. "Just don't."

"How come she can look then?" Mark asked, straining his eyes to indicate Sally, who had turned on her chair, hanging one elbow over the back to look behind her.

"Because he doesn't know her," Julia said, to Mark's confusion. "In fact, switch seats with me, Sally."

Obligingly, Sally slid from her chair and the two women squeezed past one another in order to change places, leaving Julia with her back to the pub and Sally opposite her.

Julia leaned forward onto the table and spoke in a low voice, despite the hubbub of the crowded bar. "Right, Sally, can you see behind me? A big man with a beard and arms that look like they shouldn't have fitted through the door?"

Mark shot Julia a look. "Dillon?" he asked.

Julia nodded.

Sally swivelled slightly in her seat to get a better angle. "I see him."

"What's he doing?" Julia asked.

"Coming straight towards us," Sally replied.

Julia choked down a curse and looked desperately for a means of escape, but they were cornered. A shadow fell across the table.

Julia turned and craned her neck upwards to look at Dillon as he towered over the table. She could see immediately that he'd joined the village's fast-growing lobster population, the reddened skin already peeling off across the flat expanse of his nose. A glass of cider, half full, was engulfed in one hairy hand.

He gave a quick scan of the table. "Hello, Julia. Mark." His gaze paused on Sally.

"Sally," Sally said with a pleasant smile.

"Sally," Dillon said. "Mind if I join you?"

"Whyever would we mind?" Julia said.

Dillon grabbed the back of one of the vacant chairs on the next table and dragged it across the carpet to their table before seating himself heavily on top of it.

"Because you let me think you were police officers and got me to hand over confidential information which could easily cost me my job if word got out?" Dillon said.

"Oh, you remembered that then?" Julia said.

"I take it that was you I saw hiding behind the counter in the bookshop earlier then?" Dillon said. His words were slightly slurred from the drink.

Julia nodded. "I spotted you coming and figured you'd come to give me an earful," she said.

"I had," said Dillon.

Julia braced herself. "And are you?"

"Am I what?"

"Going to give me an earful now?" said Julia.

To her surprise a smile creased up Dillon's peeling face. "Actually I've come to see the funny side of it," he said.

"Oh?" said Julia. "That's good."

"I figured that you couldn't hide in your shop forever so I went to the fête to wait you out. It turns out there was some very nice home-made cake and even nicer home-made cider."

"Home-made cider?" said Mark. "I didn't see any home-made cider."

"It sold out pretty quickly," Dillon said. "I probably helped with that."

"Ah."

"And then I found this place," Dillon said, jerking a thumb over his shoulder at the pub, "and it became harder and harder to stay angry."

"Problems do seem to lessen a bit when inside a pub," Mark agreed.

"Exactly," said Dillon, raising his glass to his lips and then wiping his beard as a thin trickle missed his lips. "And did you know that this was the pub where the rescue party for the Hurricane set out from?"

"I did hear that," Julia said.

"Which is funny," Dillon said. "Because I'd always been told it was the Barrow Arms."

Julia could only shrug.

"Anyway," Dillon said. "I know you're only trying to help Ronald and find out what happened to poor Beatrice. So as long as you can forget that I offered to hand you a bunch of laptops wanted in a police enquiry, I think I can forget too."

"Thanks," Julia said.

"Very decent of you," Mark said.

Dillon looked expectantly and slightly blearily at Sally.

"Well, ten minutes ago I didn't know that anyway," Sally said. She raised her wine glass in her hand. "So one more of these and I think I'll manage to forget all about it again."

* * *

Julia came stumbling in through the front door, far later than she had expected to. Dillon, as it turned out, was quite the chatterbox when he got going. And also quite the drinker.

Rumpkin bounded up to her as she wobbled on the doormat kicking her shoes off.

Sally appeared in the doorway behind her and leaned heavily on Julia's shoulder for support. She tapped thoughtfully at the pane of the window beside the door.

"Good grief, Mrs Burns really did come in through here for my recipe, didn't she," Sally said, running her finger over the glass.

With some effort Julia managed to disentangle herself from her pet and her housemate and turned to look. With some further effort she managed to focus too. "She really did."

"We need to teach that woman a thing or two," Sally said.

"Winning the bake-off wasn't enough?" said Julia.

Sally raised the wooden spoon which she had clutched in one hand and waved it above her head symbolically. "Not even close," Sally said, kicking the front door shut behind her and staggering onwards into the living room.

"What do you have in mind then?" said Julia as she followed. She tripped over Rumpkin and swore at him. The dog licked her hand in response.

"I don't know," Sally replied wearily, casting herself down onto the sofa with her legs dangling over the side. "But we need to put the fear of God into her."

Julia poured herself a glass of water from the kitchen tap and began drinking it. Her eyes caught sight of the cookbook lying on the shelf. The one Mrs Burns had returned to the shop. She reached up for it and on the second attempt managed to get hold of it and pull it down onto the counter.

She stared down at it. It was all blurry, but she could see the cocoa powder fingerprint was still there on the cover.

"I need to call Rhys," she said.

She dialled the number and held her phone up to her ear, swaying gently as it rang.

"Hello?"

"Jones," she said. "I mean Rhys. I'm sorry for calling so late."

There was the sound of heavy breathing down the phone. "It's only nine thirty, Julia," he said. "I haven't even got my slippers on yet."

"You never did wear the slippers I got you for your birthday," she said.

"Is that what you called to talk about?" asked Jones.

"No," Julia said. "I've got a fingerprint here. I need you to compare it to the ones you took after we had the break-in."

"You've got a fingerprint?" said Jones. "From where?"

"It's a chocolate fingerprint on a baking book," Julia said.

There was a pause from the other end of the phone.

"Hello?" Julia prompted.

"Can this wait until tomorrow, Julia?" Jones asked. "It's late and I need to get my slippers on."

"Fine," Julia replied. "But be here first thing, okay?"

"All right. I'll see you tomorrow."

"And, Rhys?"

"Yes?"

"Mark said to get you those slippers. If you don't like them it's his fault."

"Goodnight, Julia."

* * *

Julia had never been to Mrs Burns's house before. It was a nice period property located just along from the church. A converted coach house, Julia noted. One that didn't have to be demolished in order to make way for an attractive home. Jones took hold of the heavy iron ring attached to the wooden door and knocked heavily three times. Julia peered over one of his shoulders while Sally did the same on the other. They could hear a few muttering voices inside and the patter of feet before the door swung open.

Mrs Burns took the three of them in, her eyes slowly widening behind her glasses.

"Mrs Mallory Burns?" Jones intoned in a grave voice, although Julia knew that he was fully aware who she was.

She swallowed. "Yes."

There was a further pattering of footsteps within the house and a few faces appeared in the shadows of the hallway, peering out to see what was going on.

Julia recognized the reverend among them. Of course, it was the vicar's coffee morning. So this was where it was hosted. Actually, the scent of brewing coffee drifting out of the doorway stirred up something deep and primal within Julia, but she pushed those thoughts away.

Jones pulled his warrant card out and flipped it open for Mrs Burns to see. "DI Jones, King's Barrow CID. I'm afraid that it's come to light that your fingerprints have been found in the home of these two ladies following a break in."

"My... my fingerprints?" Mrs Burns stammered.

"Yes," Jones said, his voice still deadly serious. "We matched them to a book on chocolate baking which you returned to the bookstore."

"There must be some kind of mistake," Mrs Burns said.

Jones regarded her coolly. "Perhaps you have another explanation as to why your fingerprints were found at the scene of a break-in?" he said.

Mrs Burns's eyes filled with a glorious panic. "I might have wandered into the wrong house by mistake," she ventured.

Jones left a pause before replying. "Are you aware that domestic burglary carries a maximum sentence of fourteen years?" he asked.

Mrs Burns gasped, echoed by those watching from the hallway behind her. "But I didn't take anything!" she said, voice rising.

"I imagine that conspiring to win the village bake-off by nefarious means would also constitute an offence of some sort," Jones said. "Although I'd need to check with the CPS."

"You have to believe me," Mrs Burns said, reaching out towards Jones as though about to cling to his lapels before apparently thinking better of it. "I've never done anything like this before."

"Are you generally considered a woman of good standing in the community?" Jones asked.

"Oh, yes. Yes, definitely." Mrs Burns nodded her head with vigour.

"Could anyone attest to this?" said Jones.

Mrs Burns's eyes lit up. "The vicar! The vicar would speak for me."

She turned and beckoned to the vicar, and he came shuffling forwards to the doorway, glancing this way and that, managing not to meet anyone's gaze. Reaching the threshold, he cleared his throat for some time.

"Vicar," said Jones. "Would you confirm for me that you generally hold Mallory Burns to be a woman of good standing within your parish?"

The throat-clearing commenced again and eventually concluded. "Um. Yes, I would, officer."

"And can you think of any other occasions where her behaviour fell short of what might be termed exemplary."

Mrs Burns looked up at the vicar who was turning rather red. He took a deep breath. "Well..." he began.

When Jones, Julia, and Sally made their way back up the grassy slope and through the curved wooden gate the sun was noticeably higher in the sky and the church bell was chiming out the half-hour.

Jones suppressed a chuckle and once they were safely up the footpath and out of earshot he broke into a deep belly laugh. "I wasn't expecting the list to be that long," he said.

Julia smiled first at the laughing policeman and then at Sally, who had a look of quiet, if not dignified, satisfaction. "I suppose he felt that he couldn't lie," Julia said.

They carried on across the village green towards where Jones had parked his car.

"I could really use a coffee," Julia said.

* * *

Julia sat curled in the armchair as the sun started to go down outside while Rumpkin snored noisily at her feet. Sally had somehow summoned the energy to leave, begrudgingly, for work at the Barley Mow. Julia on the other hand had managed to do exceedingly little of anything all Sunday. *The Green Knight* lay open in front of her again but only a few pages had shifted over the course of the day.

Her phone rang and she made the effort to pick it up from the coffee table, more effort than she'd put into anything else for the last several hours.

She didn't really feel like talking to anyone but it was Ronald's number on the phone so she felt obliged to pick up.

"Hello, Ronald." She managed to sound less bleary than she felt.

"Hello, Julia. How are you?"

Actually, after a day of recovery, the memory of Mrs Burns's terrified face to lift her mood, and several cups of coffee, she wasn't feeling too bad now that she thought about it. "Fine, thanks," she said.

"Good. Listen, I was hoping you could come by my office tomorrow. That detective, Freiland, is hassling me again and I wouldn't mind an update on where your investigations have got to."

"Sure," Julia said, her mood dropping slightly as she reflected on the rather scant progress which she'd made so far.

"I've got a meeting with Dillon first thing. He messaged me this morning. We have some things to look over," Ronald said.

Dillon had been burning the candle at both ends. Julia knew he'd been working overtime, but after putting it away with them the day before she was impressed he'd got straight back to it today. When did he even find time to sleep? She glanced down at the pyjamas she'd already changed back into and felt a wave of shame wash over her.

"A new suspect?" Julia asked.

"No, I think he's getting somewhere working out where the money has been going," Ronald said. "Apparently it was going into an account that looked like it belonged to one of our suppliers. But the supplier says it has nothing to do with them, it was set up fraudulently. And now the police tell us the money was emptied out of there shortly after Beatrice was killed. Withdrawn in cash. It could be anywhere now. I need to assess just how bad the damage is."

Julia heard a beleaguered sigh down the telephone. She didn't envy the stress Ronald was under.

"Dillon and I will put our heads together tomorrow," he continued. "Can you come by after my meeting with him?"

"Of course."

"Wait. Actually my favourite detective is giving me a visit and after that I should probably do some work for my clients. Shall we say the end of the day? Five thirty?"

That suited Julia. At least she could close the bookshop at the normal time. "Okay," Julia replied. "We'll see you tomorrow."

Chapter 14

Julia and Mark drove past the accountancy office in the van. A silent moment passed between them and Julia could feel Mark eyeing the empty street as they went. But without raising an argument he turned off and parked down one of the side roads.

They trudged back through the puddles towards Ronald's offices. She couldn't say she was looking forward to the visit.

Ronald had asked them to give an update on their progress and in truth, Julia felt like they had very little to offer him. Mr Peabody's alibi had checked out, as had the affable Mr Tinkler's. At least as far as she was able to check it. Mr Moore was still high on Julia's list of suspects but as long as he remained low on DI Freiland's list she wasn't sure that helped Ronald much. Mr Moore's alibi was rather weak but without a way to turn the screw on him further it was enough. Julia had spent the day at the bookshop poring over the photos from his work event again but she hadn't been able to spot anything useful.

Julia pressed the bell and after a few moments Ginny answered the door. She was neatly dressed and well-groomed, as ever.

She gave them a smile. "Come on in, Ronald's expecting you, I think," Ginny said.

They followed Ginny along as she headed towards Ronald's office at the end of the corridor. As before, most of the other offices were dark and the place seemed quiet at this time in the evening. There was no sign of Gary, the intern, who was supposedly meant to answer the door. His office, such as it was, was also dark.

"Gary's knocked off early again, has he?" Julia asked.

Ginny rolled her eyes. "We had to let him go in the end. He was a nice enough chap, but just so useless. And with everything going on this wasn't the time to be carrying dead weight. Oh, that was a poor choice of words, sorry."

Julia waved the apology away as they arrived at Ronald's office. Ginny knocked smartly on the door but there was no answer. She gave Julia and Mark an apologetic look before knocking again.

"I'm sure he was here," Ginny said, frowning slightly. She turned the handle and pushed the door open a crack, peeping in.

"Hm, empty," she said. "I wonder if he went to talk to Dillon. He's been in with him a lot today. Wait here, I'll go see if they're in the IT room."

With that Ginny headed back the way they'd come, the sound of her heels clicking on the floor echoing about in the quiet office.

"It's warm in here, don't you think?" Julia asked, filling the silence.

Mark shrugged, although Julia noticed he had his jacket folded over one arm. "Perhaps they convinced Ronald to turn the thermostat up after all," he said.

"Or someone did it without him noticing," Julia said. She glanced up at the thermostat mounted on the wall, beneath the CCTV camera they had been given footage from.

Their conversation was interrupted as an ear-splitting scream came ringing down the corridor.

They spun and saw Ginny standing at the door to Dillon's office, her shaking hands held up covering her mouth. She screamed again and came running back towards them.

"They're dead, they're both dead!" Ginny said. She pointed with a trembling finger towards the half-open door.

Julia laid a comforting hand on the woman's shoulder and looked to Mark. He returned the look grimly, both knowing what they were going to have to do, both steeling themselves up for the task.

"Call an ambulance," Julia told Ginny.

She gave a rapid nod of the head and hurried off into her own office to use the phone.

With her heart pounding, Julia walked quickly towards the end of the corridor, trying to keep control of her breathing. Mark was just a couple of paces behind her.

Swallowing, Julia gave the door to the IT room a push and it swung inwards. Her eyes quickly scanned the room.

Both Dillon and Ronald lay sprawled unmoving on the floor. It was only a small space and Dillon's desk was shoved against the far wall. There were signs of a struggle there. The office chair had been thrown back, resting at an angle against the side wall with its castors in the air.

Computer parts lay littered across the desk and across the floor. At first Julia thought the computer had been hit hard enough to break it apart and send its innards scattering. As she crossed the room, she realized it was more likely Dillon had taken it apart to fix something, but still the struggle had sent the pieces tumbling onto the floor all around.

Julia skirted around Ronald's shoes to reach Dillon. He had a cable knotted around his neck – the sort used for connecting computers to the internet. She dug her fingers underneath, hoping to loosen it. It had been wrapped around tight, biting into the skin.

He was still warm, that was something, Julia told herself as she worked feverishly to try and get it off his neck – maybe there was hope.

Julia looked back over her shoulder as she worked on the cable, seeing that Mark had rolled Ronald over and was checking for a pulse. She spotted scissors lying on the floor in the pile of bits that had come off the desk and snatched them up. She slid one blade into the tiny gap under the cable that she'd manage to make with her fingers.

The cable offered more resistance than she'd predicted and she squeezed with all the force she could manage, clamping down on the scissors.

At last there was the satisfying sensation of the blades meeting and she quickly uncoiled the loop of cable from Dillon's neck and cast it aside.

Julia searched desperately for a pulse, moving her two fingers up and down the thick circle of Dillon's neck. But there was nothing. She slumped backwards, defeated, onto the thin carpet of Dillon's office and pulled her knees up to her chest.

Mark looked up at her from across the room. "I've got a pulse here," he said.

"You do?"

As if in answer, Ronald gave a groan and with pained movements he rolled over. His eyes flickered open but they had a glassy look to them.

"What happened?" he asked, his voice sounding hoarse and dry.

With Mark's help, Ronald struggled into a sitting position. Julia could see a bruise forming in a line across his forehead over his left eyebrow.

"You were attacked," Mark said. "Do you remember anything?"

Ronald massaged his temples. He was still looking about, seeming disorientated. "I came in here, I was looking for Dillon. He was meant to come by to talk to me and when he didn't I went to see where he'd got to. He was lying on the floor."

Ronald looked across the room and his eyes widened as they focussed on Dillon, lying motionless next to his desk. "Oh, no," he said.

"Let's get you to your office and we can talk there," Julia said.

She offered a hand to Ronald and between them she and Mark managed to help him to his feet. He walked, leaning heavily on them, out into the corridor. Julia tugged the door of Dillon's office closed behind them as they left.

Ginny was standing hovering at the door to her office, fingers knitting and unknitting distractedly as she watched with a pale face. "The ambulance is on its way," she said. "The police too."

"Thanks, Ginny," Julia said as they eased Ronald down the corridor.

Ginny watched them go and then looked briefly back at the closed door to Dillon's office, apparently asking and answering her own question.

As gently as they could, they lowered Ronald into the chair in his office and he sat there, breathing rapid and shallow breaths.

Ginny traipsed in, and handed a bottle of water to Ronald who managed to pour a few mouthfuls down his throat.

"Are you okay?" Ginny asked.

Ronald made a non-committal grunting sound.

"Does your head hurt?" said Ginny.

"Yeah."

Julia looked sympathetically at Ronald, noticing the welt coming up clearer now over his eye. "Do you remember who hit you?" she asked.

Ronald shook his head. "I didn't see anyone," he said. "They must have hidden behind the door or something."

"Any ideas who would have done this?" said Mark.

"No," said Ronald.

While Ginny fussed over her boss, trying to coax him to drink more water, Julia allowed herself to drift out into the corridor with Mark, where they could talk quietly to each other and still keep an eye on Ronald in his office.

"Given the cable round Dillon's neck it's safe to assume it was the same person who strangled Beatrice," Julia said.

"Which raises the question of why," said Mark.

Julia thought for a moment. "Beatrice maintained that she was innocent of the embezzlement," she said. "Which is much harder for her to prove if she's dead. Maybe someone set her up to take the fall and then killed her?"

Mark only looked puzzled. "I don't follow. Then why kill Dillon?"

"He was working through all of Beatrice's accounts," Julia said. "He might have unearthed something that our killer didn't want coming to light."

Mark scratched thoughtfully at his stubble. "It looked like there were signs of a struggle in there," he said, nodding towards Dillon's office where the IT admin had met his end. "And Dillon was no small bloke. Whoever overpowered him must have been pretty strong."

Julia cast her mind back over everyone they'd interviewed in the case. Mr Peabody she dismissed almost out of hand. Beatrice's nephew, Tony, certainly didn't look like he'd have been strong enough to tussle with someone of Dillon's imposing stature.

"What about Mr Tinkler?" Julia asked. "I did think he might have a bit of difficulty moving though."

He wasn't a particularly big man, but he had a stockiness to him that might have hidden some strength underneath it. Julia had the impression he'd not been fully mobile from the way he walked.

"He threw his back out years ago," Mark said. "He couldn't lift a sack of spuds let alone wrestle Dillon."

"I think that only leaves Mr Moore," said Julia. "Do you think he's big enough?"

"Maybe, but only just," said Mark. "Unless he knew what he was doing, it would be a risk to take on someone like Dillon, wouldn't you think?"

Julia had to agree.

Sirens began to wail outside, growing louder, soon followed by the accompanying sound of engines. She prised the blinds apart to look through as two police cars came tearing up the quiet street, tyres squealing as they came to a sudden halt outside. One was a marked car and the other a plain vehicle with a light placed on top.

She made her way to the door and pulled it open ready for the police, watching as DI Freiland hurried up the path with two uniformed constables in tow.

The detective gave Julia such a scowl as she ascended the steps that Julia shrank back away from her.

"You two," Freiland said. "I should have guessed you'd be here."

"We were seeing our client," Julia said.

"I'll bet you were," Freiland replied. She looked up and down the apparently peaceful interior of the accountancy offices. "Tell me what we've got then."

Julia pointed. "There's a body in there. Strangled. And Ronald took a bad blow to the head, he's in his office."

The detective looked to one of her constables. "Go and check on our body, I'll go and question Mr Cutty."

Julia called after Freiland as she started off towards Ronald's office. "He was attacked too. I hope you can see he's innocent in all this."

Freiland didn't bother to turn back around. "I wasn't born yesterday, Miss Ford."

Julia and Mark hurried after Freiland and her second constable as they entered the office.

Some of the colour had returned to Ronald's face and he was sitting more upright now. Either he had heard the exchange outside or he had read the unfriendly expression on Freiland's face as she came in because he remained silent and swallowed nervously.

Freiland bent to examine him, peering closely at the wound over his eyebrow.

After what felt like a hugely long stretch of time she straightened up and turned to her subordinate. "What do you think, Constable?"

The uniformed officer subjected Ronald to the same scrutiny, while the man squirmed uncomfortably under their gaze.

The policeman finished his exam. "It looks superficial to me, ma'am," he said.

"I agree. Stand up please," she said to Ronald.

Looking more and more worried by the moment, Ronald rose slowly from the chair.

Freiland reached to her hip and pulled her handcuffs free, deftly restraining Ronald's hands behind his back.

He looked too shocked to protest, so Julia did it for him. "You can't do this," she said to the detective. "That man was attacked."

DI Freiland gave a theatrical sigh. "You found him lying on the floor next to a body with a bump on his head so light my five-year-old has probably had worse while I've been at work today and won't even bother to mention it. He's hoodwinked you."

Julia gasped. "Why would he possibly do that?"

Freiland sighed again and began to explain. Julia couldn't help thinking that it might be the same tone that she used with her five-year-old.

"He killed Miss Beatrice Campbell in a fit of anger when signs of her embezzlement came to light. Dillon's been working tirelessly to root out even more of it. Not only was Mr Cutty protecting his business, but he's also hoping to cast doubt on his responsibility for the attack on Miss Campbell, as this would imply the killer was still at large."

"Do you really think Ronald could overpower someone like Dillon? He was strangled for crying out loud." Mark flapped his arm at the detective.

Freiland arched an eyebrow. "What do you mean?"

Julia felt like stamping her feet in frustration. She hadn't even gone to look at Dillon or the crime scene before pouncing on Ronald. "The man's a mountain. There's no way Ronald could wrestle him down."

Freiland paused but only for a beat. "You'd be surprised. If he took him unawares then it's certainly possible."

"Detective Freiland–" Julia said, but the detective cut her off.

"And what else are you proposing? We know Mr Cutty was at the scene of both murders. Unless you honestly think there's a mystery killer out there who is both big enough to wrestle full-grown men and small enough to scale walls and slip in through second-storey windows."

Julia opened her mouth but before she could reply Freiland was giving Ronald a steady shove between the shoulder blades to guide him out of the door.

"Read him his rights, Constable," she said. "I'm going to go and look at our victim."

Before doing so, she turned and looked at Julia and Mark. "And you two can leave, please. I know where to find you if I need you."

Julia started slowly towards the door which Freiland was holding open. "If you check the CCTV–" she began.

"I do know what I'm doing, Miss Ford," Freiland said wearily. "Unlike some of us." With that she ushered them down the corridor and towards the street.

Chapter 15

Julia sat listlessly behind the counter of the bookshop. She was rubbing her hands together to keep warm. Taking a leaf from Ronald Cutty's book, she'd turned the thermostat down a notch. Hopefully the customers wouldn't notice. When there were any.

According to Jones, Mr Moore's car hadn't gone anywhere the previous day. But that didn't prove much. Only that if he'd been to Ronald's offices, he hadn't taken his own car. She was still stewing over the fact that Freiland wouldn't bring him in for questioning.

And Jones had declined her suggestion of trumping up a charge to bring Mr Moore in on. What was the use of your boyfriend's dad being a DI if they wouldn't bend the rules for you?

Although Jones couched his words, Julia suspected that he thought Ronald had committed both murders. And by extension had been pulling Julia's strings the whole time. She only hoped that wasn't the case. If they were lucky the CCTV at Ronald's office might have picked something up. Apparently Freiland was checking it over.

The bell rang and Julia sat up attentively, trying to brighten up and smile. But it was only Mark. He looked just as miserable as she did.

"Are you on lunch already?" Julia asked, glancing at the time on her phone. "It's not even 11.30 yet."

"Mr Tinkler was on site today and he recognized me from the fête. He put two and two together that I was working with you." Mark stuck his hands in his pockets like a naughty schoolchild.

"He dismissed you?" said Julia.

"Afraid so," said Mark, scuffing at some dirt on the carpet with the toe of his boot.

"Can he do that? Don't you have a contract?"

"It's day by day," Mark said. "So, yeah, he can."

Julia frowned.

"Don't worry," Mark said. "There's always work about."

Julia rested her chin on one hand and cast an eye over the quiet shelves. "Maybe we should accept that offer to buy us out," she said. Mark was probably right about finding more work, but they really didn't need this drain on their funds.

Mark looked at her. "You can't do that," he said. "This bookshop was your dream."

Julia swept a hand around the shop, which since they had opened had gathered a lot of dust and very few customers. "That was not my dream," she said.

Once more the bell rang and this time both Julia and Mark forced on smiles only to quickly drop them again.

Jones came stomping in and came straight up to the counter. "It's cold in here," he remarked.

"What can we do for you, Rhys?" Julia said.

"Can I not just pop in to buy a book or two?" he replied.

Julia sighed. "No one else does."

Jones laid a hand on the top of her arm and gave it a gentle squeeze. "Chin up. But really I came about the case."

This at least piqued Julia's interest. "What have you found?"

"Right," said Jones. "First of all there's the CCTV footage."

"Yes?" Julia asked hopefully.

"There isn't any."

"Oh."

"It looks like someone pulled the cable out of the back of the cameras. About mid-afternoon judging by the time the feed went dark."

"Hmm. That's interesting," Mark said.

"Quite," his dad agreed. "And then there's the autopsy."

"Presumably there was one of those," said Mark.

Jones nodded. "Yes there was. And it turns out that our unfortunate IT administrator wasn't strangled."

"He wasn't?" said Julia.

"No," said Jones. "According to the coroner, the ethernet cable about his neck was put there post-mortem."

"So how did he die?" Julia asked.

"Electrocuted."

Julia's eyes widened in puzzlement. "Electrocuted? Really?"

"Yep."

Julia rested her elbows onto the counter. There was a lot to think about. "So whoever killed Dillon electrocuted him and then made it look like he was strangled."

"Presumably trying to make it look like the attacker was the same person who killed Beatrice," Mark said.

"So there are probably two killers out there," Julia said.

"You might be getting ahead of yourselves," said Jones. "I don't like to break it to you two budding detectives, but consider this. Ronald Cutty's been examined by a doctor and that head injury of his really is superficial. There's no evidence he was knocked out."

There was a glum silence until Mark spoke. "How was Dillon electrocuted?"

Jones gave an expansive shrug. "I don't know. Freiland's sent some people over to the crime scene to try and work it out. They couldn't find anything tampered with so now they think Cutty had some kind of weapon and got rid of it before he staged his own attack.

"I don't think you want to discount the possibility that he was the one who killed Dillon and then tried to make himself look like a victim too. The means of death might just be some smoke and mirrors. Or because when they find the electrical device it will point back to him so he didn't want to give a reason to go looking for it."

"You think he killed Beatrice too, don't you?" said Julia.

Jones at least had the decency to look a little sorry. "I'm just following the facts," he said. "He had the motive and he was caught on camera. I've put plenty of killers away with less when I've known in my gut they've been guilty. It would hardly be the first time someone brought PIs in to try and find someone else to pin the blame on. If nothing else it makes him look innocent by trying."

Julia couldn't meet his eye and fidgeted with her nails instead.

"Listen, I'll keep my ear to the ground. If I hear anything more, I'll let you know, all right? But don't let the fact that Cutty protests his innocence, or the fact he's employing you, sway your judgement, okay?"

"He's not employing us," Julia reminded him.

"Well, he's not paying you, but he's still your client. You know what I mean."

Jones tapped his hands on the counter by way of saying goodbye and took his leave from the shop.

"What do you think?" said Mark as the sound of his dad's car rumbled past outside the shop window.

"I think I want to get to the bottom of this," Julia said, "no matter who the killer turns out to be."

* * *

The sun was low in the sky, and irritatingly blinding whenever it emerged from the streaks of pink clouds that had banked up on the horizon. Ahead of them the earthy mass of Pagan's Hill jutted from the flat moorland. Its near flank was golden in the sunlight, the sawtooth pattern of fields emerging from the treeline standing out sharply. The cottage on the hillside was just visible, one of its windows catching the light and sparkling.

Julia and Mark were walking in silence. She turned the problems over and over in her mind without ever getting any closer to resolving them.

Around her the two dogs bounded in and out of the long grass and the yellow and pink wildflowers which had taken over this part of the fields, yapping at one another and occasionally threatening to bowl her over. But Julia was oblivious to both the danger and the beauty as she trudged onwards.

Had she really been spending all of this time unknowingly helping a murderer as he tried to wriggle off the hook? Ronald had seemed sincere enough when he came to her for help. But locally it was well known that Julia had once been in the sights of the police herself. In fact she'd done her best to advertise the fact when it looked like it would be a helpful draw for the bookshop.

So perhaps Ronald had just sensed a useful mark? Someone who would easily buy into his sob story. Julia kicked at a mole hill in frustration. It would mean that Jones was right and everything Ronald had done was just trying to distract from his heinous crimes. Hiring a PI – an unqualified one at that – sending them on some wild goose chases and then pretending he was attacked to cover up the fact he had killed Beatrice and now Dillon.

That was sloppy on Ronald's part if it was true though. Surely he knew that his head wound was going to be examined and found to be superficial? Perhaps he hadn't had the backbone to fully go through with it. Or perhaps he just had more confidence in his acting skills than they merited.

Julia sighed and for the first time on the walk stopped to look out over the moors and listen to the sound of the dogs playing and the birds singing. A few fields over, a tractor made its tireless path up and down, furrowing the ground. She should have spent the walk looking for that missing dog rather than stewing on Ronald's case, Julia thought bitterly. It might have been a better use of her time. She probably had a better chance of solving that case.

As she stood and pondered, her phone went off and she opened up her handbag to retrieve it. She didn't recognize the number and hesitated before she answered it.

"Hello?" she said cautiously, resuming her walk through the grass.

"Miss Ford!" Julia recognized Ronald on the other end of the line. The strain in his voice was plain to hear. "Thank goodness I got through to you."

"Hi, Ronald," Julia replied. "What can I do for you?"

"I need your help," he said. "The police are throwing everything they can at me to see what sticks and the duty solicitor here seems intent on doing as little as he possibly can."

"I thought you had your own lawyer," Julia said. The memory of having to deal with the duty solicitor when he was defending her made her shudder.

"I did, until the money ran out," Ronald said. "It turns out if all your money is in a business and that business is embroiled in an embezzlement case then lawyers tend to want paying up front."

"What is it you want me to do?" Julia asked.

"Something. Anything," said Ronald. "My new solicitor, legal mastermind that he is, just wants me to plead guilty. But I didn't do it. Earlier they said I tampered with the office electrics and then when they couldn't find anything they said I made some sort of taser and then hid it. I can't do any of that, I get someone in to do anything more complicated than changing a light bulb."

Julia frowned as she walked. Not that he was necessarily telling the truth, but jerry-rigging some kind of taser weapon did seem rather far-fetched.

"I'll do what I can, but I'm not sure what I can really do to help," Julia said.

"I'm sure you'll think of something," Ronald said. "Look, I have to go. But thank you for helping me. You're really my only hope."

The line went dead and Julia shoved her mobile back into her pocket.

"What did he want?" said Mark, hurrying to keep up. Julia's pace had quickened as she was talking.

"He wanted help," Julia said, filling him in as they walked. The afternoon was getting on now and the air was quickly beginning to cool but the anger driving her pace kept her from getting cold.

"I appreciate you wanting to help, but what can we do?" Mark asked.

"I don't know yet," Julia said, trudging onwards.

First the police thought Dillon's office was booby-trapped. Then they thought that there was some kind of taser involved. But in both cases they fancied Ronald as the culprit. It seemed that the police were going to turn whatever facts they could find against him. And if he really had done it, there wasn't going to be any harm in trying to prove otherwise, was there?

Without warning she turned on her heel and started marching back towards the car.

"Come on," she called to the dogs. They roundly ignored her, having fun exploring the undergrowth, but Mark came faithfully trailing behind her.

"What is it?" he asked.

"We need to take a look at Dillon's office for ourselves," she said, glancing over at Mark as he caught up. "I can't believe Ronald was running around with an improvised taser. If something was tampered with there, the police must have missed it."

Mark smiled. "Let me fetch a few things from the van," he said.

Chapter 16

It was dark by the time Julia and Mark arrived in King's Barrow. The network of streets behind Ronald's offices were narrow, oddly laid out and poorly lit. But luckily they'd had some experience finding their way around them by now, and they had little trouble getting to the back of the building rather than the front.

Luckier still, the back of the building was right next to the pavement so they didn't have to worry about scaling any gates or fences. The downside, of course, was that if anyone did happen to pass by they would be in full view. Julia had dressed all in black for the occasion, digging out her little-used running gear for the task: a black zip-up hoodie and black Lycra bottoms. Mark had branded that silly, saying it would only make them look more suspicious. He wore a nondescript light-grey hoodie with jeans.

Thinking about it now, as she stood there with a flathead screwdriver in one hand, Julia realized they had chosen the worst of both worlds: he was easy to spot and she looked suspicious. Perhaps she could pass herself off as a jogger, as long as no one expected her to actually run more than about five paces.

She looked along the building, trying to get her bearings. They had ruled out going through the back entrance which led directly into what had been the sorry little office belonging to Gary. Their quick look at it on their first visit had suggested it only opened from the inside, and discussing on the drive over they thought it would likely be alarmed anyway, being the fire escape. Instead, they'd decided that going through the window directly into Dillon's office was their best hope of getting in without being spotted.

"This will be it," Mark said, looking up.

The sash window was set high up in the wall, the bottom of it about level with Julia's collarbone. She gave an inward sigh. Things were never straightforward.

"Boost me up," she said.

"Here we go," Mark replied, cupping his hands together for her.

She wobbled up into the air, leaning one hand against the windowsill for support and working the screwdriver into the join with the other. Thank goodness Ronald had gone for a period property. There was no chance of doing this successfully on a modern window. Julia made a mental note to talk to her landlord about that.

After spending a few fruitless minutes trying to jam the screwdriver into a gap that didn't seem to exist, Julia gave up and lowered herself back to the pavement.

"You try," she said to Mark, handing him the screwdriver.

"Someone's coming," he hissed, grabbing Julia and pressing his lips to hers.

She allowed herself to hang loosely off him, keeping her eyes open. She saw a middle-aged woman make her way past on the far pavement, giving them an odd look as she passed by before turning the corner and disappearing.

She roughly shoved Mark away. "It's dark enough here, I don't think she would have even seen us if you just stayed still," she said.

"More fun that way though," Mark said. In spite of the darkness Julia knew he was grinning.

"Go on and get that window open," she instructed.

Being slightly taller, Mark could just reach the window by standing on his tiptoes, albeit awkwardly. For a few minutes he stood there grunting and occasionally swearing as he poked at it with the screwdriver.

"It's no good," he said eventually, coming down off his tiptoes and patting the end of the screwdriver in his palm thoughtfully. How Mrs Burns had managed this at her house was lost on Julia.

"We could break the window," Mark said.

Julia shook her head vigorously. "That will draw way too much attention," she said. It may be quiet in the street but there were houses all around.

"Is there anyone who might let us in?" Mark asked, looking carefully up and down at the building as though a window might open on its own accord if he studied it hard enough.

"Probably not, with Ronald banged up," Julia said. "Up until yesterday I'd have said Dillon might have been worth a shot," she added, a touch sadly.

"What about Ginny?" said Mark.

Julia considered that for a moment. "We don't know her that well," she said. "She might refuse. Or worse, tell Freiland."

"I reckon it's worth a shot," said Mark.

She couldn't think of any better ideas. "Fine," Julia said, reaching for her phone.

The phone rang a few times. Julia had been hoping that she might not pick up and then she could go home and forget about the whole escapade. But just as she was sure it would go to answerphone, Ginny picked up.

"Hi," Julia said, trying to sound as casual as she could. "We were hoping to take another look in the office and see if there's anything we missed. Is there any chance you could pop by and let us in?"

"Do you want to come by tomorrow morning? It's only Dillon's office that's off limits. We're still working as normal in the rest," Ginny said.

"That's kind of the thing…" Julia said.

There was a long silence on the other end of the phone and then she heard Ginny take a deep intake of breath. "Sorry, I'm really not sure I should. I could get into trouble if the police found out."

The woman was obviously nervous, that Californian edge creeping back into her accent.

Julia didn't like to turn the screw but this might be their only shot at looking into Dillon's office before the police turned it inside out looking for this sci-fi weapon of theirs, so she persisted. "If you just came by and dropped the key to us," she said. "You wouldn't need to come inside."

There was an even longer pause. Then to Julia's surprise Ginny agreed. "Okay," she said. "I'll hand you the key. But you never got it from me, okay?"

Julia smiled. "Deal," she said.

* * *

Ten minutes later, Julia and Mark were waiting a few doors down from the front of the building, leaning against the iron railings of another converted office.

They straightened up when they heard footsteps approaching from down the street. Ginny was wearing a black jumper with the hood pulled up. Mark was right, Julia thought, it did make her look suspicious, actually.

She didn't greet them when she arrived, but rather looked nervously this way and that as though the police might be lurking in any shadow.

Apparently satisfied that they were alone, Ginny reached a hand into her pocket and pulled the office key out, holding it towards them. "Don't forget, this wasn't from me," she said.

"Don't worry," Julia said, palming the key. "It won't lead back to you. We'll drop it through your letter box when we're done."

"And don't get caught," Ginny said.

"We won't," Mark assured her.

With that, Ginny turned and with quick footsteps disappeared back the way she'd come.

Julia exchanged a look with Mark. "Let's get going then," she said.

As they made the short walk to the front of Ronald's offices, Julia peered up at the spot above the door. Even knowing it was there, the CCTV camera was hard to spot. Hopefully it was still out of action but, not wanting to take any chances, she flipped her own hood up and kept her head down as she unlocked the front door and stepped inside.

The corridor, which had seemed so bland and sanitized before, was unnerving now it was after dark, with only the distant streetlight trickling in and casting shadows about the place. But Julia didn't dare turn the light on. Who knew if the police were keeping tabs on this place.

Their footsteps echoed as they made their way to the end of the corridor to the door to Dillon's office, sounding far louder than they should have.

A web of police tape criss-crossed the doorway. With an uncomfortable amount of familiarity, Julia allowed Mark to pull two of the strands apart so she could duck through into Dillon's room.

The blinds were drawn on the front window and the other window, the one that they had unsuccessfully tried to enter through, only looked out on the back street, so Julia risked turning the light on. It wasn't like they were going to find anything groping around in the darkness.

She blinked as the room came into view. It was much as it had been when they had last seen it, minus Dillon's body, of course. Some of the computer parts remained strewn about the desk and floor while others had been taken away. Julia couldn't have said why the police had taken some of them, but presumably they had their reasons.

"What now?" asked Mark.

Now they were there, Julia wasn't quite sure what she was hoping to find.

She glanced about for a second then crossed to the far side of the room. "Let's start where the body was," she said to Mark, keeping her voice down although if anyone else was in the building they would probably already know she and Mark were there.

Julia followed Mark to the far wall, and they both crouched down on their haunches at the approximate spot where they had found Dillon.

"Look here," Mark said. He pointed with the tip of the screwdriver at a plug socket on the wall there. It was made of a mock brass that glinted in the light.

"Could that have electrocuted him?" Julia asked. She hoped that even the King's Barrow police, who she held in fairly low esteem, would have checked the outlet.

Mark shrugged and fumbled in the bulging pocket of his hoodie for the multimeter he'd brought along.

"Careful," Julia hissed.

Mark ignored her and attached the probes to the holes in the socket. "It's a perfectly normal outlet," he said.

Julia let her breath out slowly.

Mark tapped at the faceplate with his finger. "Look at this though."

Julia leaned in close to examine it, still slightly wary that it might somehow still shock her if she touched it. "What about it?" she asked.

There were two screws fixing the socket to the wall, one on either side. "This one isn't screwed in quite as deeply as the other," Mark said, indicating one of them. "I think it's a bit loose."

He pulled a small crosshead screwdriver out and gave it a poke. "It is loose," he said. "Whoever last put this on must have been in a hurry. Let's have a look."

He set to work unscrewing the faceplate and eased it from the wall. "Ha!" Mark exclaimed. "I think I was right."

Julia looked at the socket dangling from the wall by the coloured wires. Whatever Mark had spotted was eluding her and it was beginning to frustrate her now. "What?" she said.

Mark pointed at something with the tip of the screwdriver. Julia didn't try to stop him this time, it would serve him right if he got shocked.

"The live wire's been rewired back in in a hurry," he said. "It's a rush job."

They all looked much the same to Julia, but she took Mark's word for it. "But why?" she asked.

"Look here," Mark said.

This time Julia could see what he was pointing out. There was a small hole drilled into the black plastic backing, only the width of one of the wires. It was slightly rough round the edges, obviously done by hand and not part of the manufacturing.

"Someone connected the live wire up to the switch," Mark said.

"So when Dillon touched it…" Julia said.

Mark nodded. "It shocked him."

"And then whoever did it put it back afterwards," Julia said.

"But not particularly well," Mark added.

They were interrupted when there was a loud squeal of tyres outside on the road and they both looked round.

Julia pushed herself to her feet and hurried across the room, making a tiny slit in the blinds to peek out from. "It's the police," she said, watching as the car doors opened.

"My dad?" Mark asked hopefully.

"Not unless he recently started wearing blouses and trouser suits," Julia said, hurrying back away from the window in case she was spotted.

Mark was already undoing the clasp on the rear window. "Let's go," he said.

Julia glanced at the socket hanging from the wall. She shoved it back into place and tightened the screws as best she could by hand.

"Just leave it," Mark said in a harsh whisper. "Hurry up."

Julia finished with the socket and stood up. "What if they're out the back as well? We'll walk straight into them," she said.

"I'll take my chances," Mark said, lifting the sash window and hooking one leg through. He looked at Julia imploringly. "Come on."

Julia stood for a moment more in indecision, but as she heard the front door opening she ran over to Mark.

He slid down from the window onto the pavement outside and held his arms up for Julia.

She swung her legs out and felt him grab her by the hips and help slow her descent as she came down. As her shoes touched the asphalt she could hear voices inside the room they'd just come from, including Freiland's. There was no time to close the window now.

She felt Mark tugging on her arm and she turned and joined him as they ran down the pavement.

A voice called after them to stop. They were already rounding the corner now, hurrying into the dimly lit street beyond.

Julia didn't dare look back but she could hear a pair of feet echoing after them. From that distance, they must have seen which way they'd gone.

"This way," Mark said, pulling her down the next turning.

They came skidding to a halt. It wasn't another street that they'd run into, just a narrow alleyway between houses that quickly ended in a brick wall.

Julia glanced back and considered making a break for it but the pursuing footsteps were almost upon them now. At least the alleyway was dark. They pushed themselves flush into the shadows and Julia did her best to still her heavy breathing. She felt Mark's fingers lock around her own.

A uniformed policeman came pelting past the alley entrance, carrying on down the street, the sound of their footfalls gradually dying away.

Julia let out a rasping breath. "Too close," she said.

Mark nodded and pulled her close, wrapping an arm around her.

Someone at the entrance to the alley cleared their throat and Julia and Mark both looked up.

The woman who had passed them on the street before was looking at them down her nose. "Get a room," she hissed, before continuing on her way.

Julia disentangled herself from Mark. "Let's get out of here," she whispered.

* * *

The police were waiting for them when they arrived back at Julia's house. Luckily it was in the form of Mark's dad.

Jones was sitting on their sofa, next to Sally, and sipping tea from a cup. With slow, deliberate movements he placed the cup onto the saucer and the saucer onto the coffee table when they arrived.

"I was wondering when you two would show up," he said.

Julia shuffled her feet sheepishly.

"You do know that Freiland knows precisely what you've been up to?" Jones continued.

"Ah, but can she prove it?" Mark asked.

"She doesn't need to prove it to take you in for questioning," Jones said. "I only just talked her down from it by saying it would be a waste of resources. But her patience is going to run out pretty soon. I would think carefully before your next move."

"And next time you commit a break-in, please don't take my car," Sally added.

"But my van's got my name all over it," Mark said.

Sally scowled at him.

"Well, come on then, what did you find out?" Jones asked. "Anything?"

Standing felt too much like being in the headmaster's office again so Julia lowered herself into the armchair, even if that left poor Mark standing on his own.

She briefly told Jones what they had found in Dillon's office, with the plug socket that looked like it had been sabotaged.

"And whoever did it tidied up after themselves," Julia concluded.

Jones blinked slowly and then fixed Julia a stare. "Well you know who had the prime opportunity to do that, don't you, Julia?"

Julia sighed deeply. "You mean Ronald," she said.

"Exactly," Jones said. "He could have laid his trap and after Dillon had been shocked he could have cleared up and then thrown himself to the ground pretending the two of them had been assaulted."

"Although with the CCTV turned off, anyone could have covered up after themselves and left," Julia added quickly.

"They could have," Jones said. "But they'd have risked being discovered at any point while they were doing it and making their exit. They'd have to have been very lucky or very careful."

With that he rose from the sofa, an act which took no small amount of time and effort. "I've said it before," he said. "You need to be careful. You're on the verge of annoying Freiland beyond the point of no return. And even if you don't, there's a good chance all you're doing is unwittingly helping the real culprit. The evidence against Ronald is stacking up." He nodded briefly to Sally. "Thanks for the tea," he said. "I'll see myself out."

"Your dad is probably right," Julia said to Mark as the door clicked shut behind Jones. "Ronald is the obvious culprit, isn't he? He's just played me for a fool the whole time."

"No, there are still bits that don't add up," Mark insisted. Whether he truly believed that or just wanted to buck her spirits up, Julia wasn't sure. Or maybe he just defaulted to disagreeing with his father.

Whatever the reason, he seemed quite animated as he continued. "Why would he fling himself onto the floor after electrocuting Dillon? Do you know what I think happened?"

"What?" Julia asked, annoyed that he didn't just say. Maybe a little annoyed at the world in general.

"I think someone electrocuted Dillon and then Ronald came in before they had time to cover their tracks. The killer, whoever they were, hid behind the door just like Ronald thought.

"So Ronald goes into Dillon's office and sees him lying prone on the floor. What did we do in that situation? We rushed forward to help, to check for a pulse and so on. Ronald probably did the same. And as soon as he touched Dillon: zzzppt" – Mark mimed receiving an electric shock – "and Ronald's fired back across the room. He takes a small bump to the head in the process, but falling unconscious is from the shock, not the knock.

"The killer gets their chance to tidy up their booby trap before they escape, but they have to rush because they don't know how long Ronald will be out for. When he does come back around, the last thing he remembers is going to help Dillon, so of course he assumes someone clonked him on the head."

Julia nodded along as Mark was speaking. It made sense. The bump on Ronald's head was so slight no one would have believed it would have stunned him. And the killer had never intended for the police to work out that Dillon was killed by an electric shock.

At least, Julia thought, not unless Ronald was several moves ahead.

Chapter 17

Sally went out early the next morning to get tea bags. They'd been deemed essential. While she was out, Julia made quick use of Sally's printer, hoping to get away with not reimbursing her for the ink. She supposed this was the sort of thing that PIs claimed under expenses. Real PIs that was.

She carefully carried the A4 sheets downstairs, still wet with ink. She took the photos of Beatrice, Ronald, Dillon and Brad Moore and pinned them up on the corkboard by the fridge, leaving the rest of the printouts in a stack on the counter beside the board in case she needed them later.

Mark floated in from the living room and looked the corkboard up and down. "All you're missing is some red string to connect them all," he said.

There was some string in the drawer, Julia thought. And some red food colouring in the top cupboard.

"No, stay focused," Julia chided herself and turned her attention back to the board.

The list of suspects was depressingly slender.

Mr Moore's photo she had printed off from his website and he looked rather dapper and unthreatening. Despite this he was Julia's prime suspect and as such he was placed accordingly in the prime spot at the top of the noticeboard, covering up the shopping list. He was small enough to gain entry to Beatrice's flat via the window. Plus he had motive if he had discovered his missing money and his alibi on the night of Beatrice's murder was flimsy.

For now though, Julia couldn't think why he would have wanted to kill Dillon. If he had been strangled, then perhaps Mr Moore had broken in looking for some clue where his money had gone and Dillon had disturbed him in the act.

But that didn't make sense with the booby-trapped wall socket, obviously planned in advance.

Just beneath his photo, Julia had pinned a picture of Ronald.

She had listened to what Jones had said and not wholly discounted Ronald. He was the one person known to be at the scene of both murders. But the police were investigating him and surely it would be unethical of Julia to investigate her own client.

The list of suspects was a bit meagre but on the stack she hadn't pinned up yet, Julia had photos for all the other employees at the accountancy firm, taken from the staff webpage. Someone had cut the CCTV off earlier in the day when Dillon was killed which suggested someone who worked there.

Julia hopped up onto the kitchen counter opposite and looked at the photo of Dillon. A plan slowly began to crystallize in her mind. Maybe she could send Sally in to poke around the accountancy firm employees. They wouldn't recognize her, so with a suitable excuse she could probably get herself inside and get talking to people, seeing if there was any gossip.

That would free herself and Mark up to dig further into Mr Moore's movements after their previous, unsuccessful, operation. He lived alone, but with a house and garden that big he must have a cleaner or a gardener or something. Maybe one of them saw him leave on the night of Dillon's murder.

Julia was still sitting there deep in thought when the front door banged and a few moments later Sally came pottering in, an armful of shopping hugged to her chest.

"I forgot the bag for life," she said, depositing the groceries next to Julia.

Sally saw Julia's look of deep concentration and turned to see the requisitioned corkboard on the wall facing her.

"Why do you have a picture of the skank?" she asked.

Julia looked at her friend, puzzled. "Huh? Who?"

Sally tapped the photo of Ginny. "Her."

"And what makes you say that?" said Julia.

"Well, I saw her with her tongue halfway down Mr Tinkler's throat at the fête," said Sally. "Anyone who can stomach being so close to that sleazebag is obviously a skank."

Julia leaned forward and steepled her fingers under her chin. "Really?" she said.

"Yep. I saw them when I was heading to the kitchen to put my cake in the freezer. For all the good that did. So who is she?"

"Her name's Ginny Stroup," Julia replied. "She's an accountant at Ronald Cutty's company."

"You didn't know that she knew Mr Tinkler then?" said Sally.

"Oh, I knew that they knew each other," Julia said. "I was told that Ginny disliked Mr Tinkler so much that she had to be removed from handling his account."

"They looked friendly enough to me," Sally said.

162

Julia's eyes widened and she looked at Mark. "You don't think that she was the one…" She trailed off as her mind raced away faster than her mouth could cope.

"The one who took my cake out of the freezer?" said Sally.

Julia made an exasperated noise at her friend. "No. The one who killed Beatrice," she said. She slid from the counter and began pacing the tiny kitchen.

"Are you sure?" said Sally. "I think you might be underestimating how seriously people took that bake-off. You didn't believe Mrs Burns had broken into our house for my recipe either."

Julia was ignoring her now. She was lost too deep in thought as she tried to make sense of it all. Why would Ginny have lied about knowing Mr Tinkler? She was in the room when Ronald joked about how much Ginny disliked him. She obviously didn't want their relationship to be public knowledge, even if they'd allowed themselves to get carried away at the village fête they'd still hidden themselves away from prying eyes. Or they thought they had.

"Go on then, what are you thinking?" Mark asked.

Julia ceased her pacing and strode past her friend and into the living room, looking about for her laptop. Mark and Sally followed on her heels.

"I think," she said, somewhat distractedly, "that this means Ginny and Mr Tinkler have been working together the whole time.

"They embezzled the money and pinned it on Beatrice. They killed her to stop her clearing her name. Then they killed Dillon. I'm guessing his digging must have been getting close to something and they needed to stop it."

"Hang on, hang on," Mark said as Julia lifted each of the sofa cushions in turn. "Why would they steal money from Mr Tinkler's company? It was already his money."

"But it's not." Julia stopped to look at Mark. "It's the company's money, he couldn't just take it. He'll have partners. And people he owes money to."

"Hm, fair enough," said Mark.

Julia went down on all fours to inspect underneath the coffee table.

"What are you looking for anyway?" said Sally.

"My laptop," Julia said, clambering back to her feet. "I can see why Ginny and Mr Tinkler might have killed Beatrice but we'd still need to work out how."

Julia's finger shot into the air. "I've got it!"

Sally bounced excitedly, swept up in Julia's enthusiasm. "How did they do it then?"

"No, I mean I've remembered that I left my laptop in your room," Julia said, sweeping from the lounge and pounding up the stairs.

"Why?" Sally called after her.

"Not important," Julia called back. After a short pause she came thumping down the stairs again.

"What exactly are you looking for?" Sally asked as Julia dumped the laptop onto the coffee table and pushed the lid open, sitting down on the sofa in front of it.

"Let me find it," Julia said. She tapped at the keys until she brought up the CCTV image she had of Ginny from the footage Ronald had sent.

Julia pointed at the screen. "Look, no gloves," she said triumphantly.

"What?" Sally peered over Julia's shoulder.

"When we saw Ginny after Beatrice had died, she had been wearing gloves in the office because of the cold. But this image was taken the night Beatrice was killed, during the cold snap, and she's not wearing them."

"Which means?" Sally prompted.

Julia mimed garrotting someone with a kettle cord. "Which means I think she was hiding her hands. They were bearing marks from when she strangled Beatrice."

"So it was her," Mark said.

Julia frowned as she looked at the grainy image once more, making certain about the gloves. "It still doesn't explain how she got into the flat unnoticed."

Sally sat herself down next to Julia. "Show me the doorbell photos," she said.

"Okay," Julia said, tapping on the keyboard once more. "But I've really scoured over them. I don't think I've missed anything."

Sally took up the laptop and thoughtfully flicked back and forwards through the photos a couple of times, her face glowing in the light from the screen. "You're missing one," she said.

"What do you mean?" said Julia.

Sally passed the laptop over. "Look at the filenames," she said. "Each name is the date the photo was taken with a number after it. The postman was photo one. Then Ronald Cutty is two. But the police are number four. Where did three go?"

Julia stared at the list of files on the screen. "You're right," she said. "Someone must have deleted it."

"Presumably someone knew there was something incriminating on there," Mark said. "But who would have access to them? You said Beatrice's nephew set this up?"

"He did, but I don't think that's who deleted the photo. Even I could guess the password that Beatrice used. And apparently she used to stick Post-it notes with her passwords to her work monitor."

"Ah. So Ginny would have guessed too," said Sally.

"Exactly."

"One question then," said Mark. "Why did Beatrice give Ronald's name on the 999 call? Was she calling him for help? Would he still have been outside?"

"No. At the very least Ginny must have waited while he cleared off down the steps or he would have seen her." Julia thought for a moment then snapped her fingers. "That recording. I knew there was something bothering me about it."

She plugged the memory stick back into the laptop and played the file again. Now she knew what she was listening for it was clear as day.

"I don't get it," Sally said. "What can you hear?"

"Listen to the way she says 'Cutty'," said Julia. "I thought it didn't sound right. Everyone thought it was because Beatrice was struggling to breathe. But those 't's sound like 'd's. That's an American accent. A faint one. The one Ginny lapses into sometimes. Including, apparently, when she's full of adrenaline."

Sally nodded. "The icing on the cake to frame Cutty then," she said.

Julia allowed herself to collapse back into the cushions of the sofa. She was convinced. "None of this will stand up in court, though," Julia said, staring at the ceiling. "A photo which isn't there, no gloves on a cold day, and a slightly off pronunciation on the 999 call."

"What about Dillon's murder? Maybe we could get them on that?" suggested Mark.

Julia grunted. Ginny would certainly have had the opportunity both to booby-trap the socket in Dillon's office and to cover her tracks afterwards. With Mr Tinkler's experience in construction he could surely have told her what to do.

But any number of other workers at the office would have had the chance as well. At the very least it would be enough for Ginny to cast doubt.

"If they stick to their story there's no hard evidence against them. I think we need to flush them out," Julia said.

"What have you got in mind?" Mark asked.

"I'm not sure yet. We need to make them think we're onto them. The money's still missing, Ronald said it had been withdrawn as cash now. I'm guessing they've squirrelled it away somewhere. That's surely why they felt they had to kill Dillon. He was too close to connecting the fraudulent account to Ginny. If we can make them think we're closing in, maybe they'll go for their cash."

"And do what?" Sally said.

Julia bit her lip thoughtfully. "Well, Mr Tinkler is a keen traveller. He claims he hates the climate here. I wouldn't be surprised if their plan was to abscond out of the country with their cash once the heat died down."

"So how do we make them think we're onto them?" Sally asked.

"We need to trick them," Julia said. "And I think I know who might be able to help us."

* * *

Julia watched Jones's face from across his living room, waiting for any kind of sign as to what the detective was thinking. He was still studying the photo that Julia had given him a few minutes before when she had set about explaining her plan.

Sensing her nervousness, Mark gave Julia's hand a gentle, reassuring squeeze.

At long last, Jones lowered the photo and let it fall into his lap, revealing a deeply unimpressed face.

"It's a blooming stupid idea, Julia," he said.

"I know that," she replied. "But will it work?"

"You could get hurt," Jones said.

"That's not what I asked."

Jones gave an exasperated snort through his nose, setting the white bristles of his moustache twitching. "It might do," he conceded.

Julia couldn't help herself from grinning.

"At the very least I don't see it doing any harm," said Jones. "To the case, I mean, rather than to you. If you've got the wrong person you won't get any reaction other than maybe getting egg on a few faces. Since you seem adamant on going through with it anyway it's probably foolish of me to try and talk you out of it."

"But if I have got the right person," Julia prompted.

With some effort Jones stretched forwards to hand the photo back to Julia. "If Ginny really was involved, then I expect you'll get a reaction, yes."

Chapter 18

Julia sat perched on one of the high stools in Biddle Rhyne's café, blowing on the oversized mug of coffee and studying the decorative swirls in the frothed milk.

Ginny was late. Perhaps she wouldn't come. If she had the sense to keep her trap firmly shut then there wasn't a lot that Julia could do.

Then again, as far as Ginny knew, Julia still had the wool firmly pulled down over her eyes and was floundering about trying to prove Ronald's innocence, chasing down one embezzled customer after another. So perhaps Ginny was just stuck in traffic.

Julia looked across the room at the window facing onto Biddle Rhyne's high street. Jones sat huddled at the corner table, obscured by a broadsheet paper that he had unfolded in front of him. She still couldn't help thinking that he liked playing the role of spy a little too much.

Behind him there was indeed a line of cars, almost stationary, creeping forward.

As Julia watched, the café door was pushed open and Ginny entered. She was smartly dressed, as usual, and smiled at Julia as she weaved among the tables. She was certainly cool under pressure, Julia could give her that.

"Hello," Ginny said pleasantly as she took the seat opposite Julia and placed her handbag up on top of the small metal table. "Sorry I'm late, traffic was just, urgh." She rolled her eyes and fluttered her fingers in the air.

"Yes, it can be like that around here," Julia said, half on autopilot as her heart raced away inside her chest.

"Anyway," Ginny said, "you said that you had my key to give back."

Julia opened her own handbag. Instead of Ginny's key she pulled a printed photo out, holding the sheet of A4 just above the bag.

Ginny's eyes widened as she saw it and leaned in for a better look.

Julia knew the timing was crucial, she couldn't let Ginny examine it too closely.

Mr Moore was a whizz at Photoshop, but he could only work with what he had. And what he had was the CCTV still of Ginny leaving work on the day of Beatrice's murder. Julia could only hope she wore the same clothes when she rang the doorbell at Beatrice's, or at the very least didn't consciously change them.

It had taken Mr Moore a surprisingly short amount of time to impose that on the background of the doorbell photos that Julia did have. She supposed that getting the PI accusing you of murder out of your hair was as good a motivator as any.

Before Ginny could examine the doctored photo too thoroughly, Julia shoved it back into the depths of her handbag and then clipped the bag shut primly. She did her best to look Ginny in the eye and was pleased to detect some hints of worry in there finally.

"So," Julia said.

"But I—" Ginny started and then checked herself, clamping her mouth shut. "Where did you get that?" she said instead, after a pause.

"I'd prefer not to say," Julia said. "By the way, how are your hands healing up? You know, when I look closely I think I can still see a mark."

Ginny slid her hands off the table and onto her lap. "What do you want?" she said.

"My client is innocent," said Julia. "I think we both know that."

Ginny remained quiet, so Julia continued. "My methods of obtaining this evidence were not, in the strictest sense, legal. And I'd prefer not to stick my own neck out by handing it over. But I'm not going to let an innocent man go to prison for murder. I'll take my own little fall, if I have to.

"So here's what I'm going to do. I'll give you twenty-four hours to turn yourself in to the police. After that I'll do it myself, and what happens, happens. If they charge me with something too, I'll live with it."

Ginny swallowed and continued her silence.

Julia took a sip from her drink, hoping her hand wasn't shaking too much. "Mmm," she said. "Did you want to get one too? The queue's starting to build up."

In reply, Ginny swept her handbag up and hurried quickly from the café, looking a little unsteady on her heels.

Julia watched her leave with quiet satisfaction.

As the door closed itself quietly on the traffic outside, Jones lowered his paper and gave Julia a knowing look across the intervening table before getting up and following Ginny out.

* * *

Julia forced herself to finish her coffee even though every nerve was screaming at her to grab her stuff and race after Ginny. Her heart was still pumping manically, but she knew the plan was a good one. Let Jones tail her discreetly and see if she contacted Mr Tinkler and used their twenty-four hours head start to grab the money and bug out.

If they did so then Jones could swoop in and arrest them.

Julia pushed the empty cup away and walked through the door, heading up the short section of the high street to the bookshop.

Mark was waiting behind the counter. He looked equally agitated. "How did it go?" he asked.

"Everything went fine," Julia said. "Now we just need to see what she does."

Unable to keep still, Julia strode around the bookshop dusting the shelves. Then, when she was done, Mark went round and dusted them properly.

Just as he was finishing up, Julia's phone rang and she snatched it out of her handbag. It was Jones.

"Yes?" Julia asked. Mark leaned in to listen, almost bumping heads, so Julia put the mobile to speakerphone and put it on the counter.

"I lost her," Jones said.

Julia felt her knees go weak. She could have screamed.

Jones's monotone voice crackled over the speaker. "I followed her home and then about two minutes later she drove off again. She headed north out of King's Barrow. It looked like she turned off the A-road around Shellback Hill and I lost her on the lanes. I couldn't risk getting too close without being obvious."

"I know where she was going," said Mark.

"Where?" Julia and Jones both spoke at the same time.

"That's where Mr Tinkler's job site is," he said.

"I'll head there now, I think I know the place," Jones said.

Mark looked to Julia.

"Let's get to the van," she said.

* * *

Mark guided the van as it bounced on its suspension down the dirt and gravel track.

The building site was expansive. It was hard to tell how many homes were being put up in total since they were all at different stages of construction. But what had recently been a farmer's field was now levelled and covered mostly in tarmac. A handful at the far end looked to be finished, as far as Julia could tell, and the footprints of several more buildings were marked out by incomplete brick walls. Great spools of piping and cabling were piled all around with little apparent order to them. The sound of power tools and vehicles moving filled the air.

Mark pulled up somewhere on the edge of the site, where several other trade vans were lined up.

As Mark slammed the van door after him, a builder in a high-vis vest standing at the edge of the parking area looked up from the clipboard he was holding.

"Jones? I thought we got rid of you," he said.

It was hard to tell if he was joking or not. He certainly had the look of someone who'd had about enough of Mark's sense of humour as they could stomach. Julia had learned to recognize it well.

However serious it was meant to be, Mark ignored the jibe. "Is Mr Tinkler here?" he said, peering out at the movement on the construction site.

"Yeah, over in one of the finished builds I think. Why?"

Mark motioned to Julia. "Come on, let's go."

They broke into a run across the uneven ground but they only got a couple of paces when a voice behind them made them stop.

"Hey." Despite being only a single word, Julia could hear the Welsh accent in it.

She turned and saw Jones hurrying over the mud from the site entrance, struggling towards them as fast as he could manage, his tie flapping behind him and his face turning red.

A few moments later he'd caught them up. Leaning heavily on his thighs as he caught his breath, huffing and wheezing as he spoke, he said, "Just what are you two doing?"

Julia blinked. "We're going after them," she said, motioning vaguely in the direction of the completed homes where she understood that Ginny and Mr Tinker had headed.

Jones shook his head. "We're meant to be laying a trap remember? What if they've seen you? Trundling up in that great van of yours?" He flapped a hand at Mark's vehicle.

Julia and Mark looked sheepishly at one another. The man had a point.

"I can move it if you like," Mark said.

"No point now," said Jones, his breathing returning to something close to normal. "If they haven't noticed it already then they're more likely to if you start pootling it around the car park."

"Where have you been? We thought you got lost," Julia said.

"There's only one entrance," Jones pointed out. "Unless they plan on scaling the security fence and disappearing off over the fields, they're coming out the same way they came in. Hopefully with whatever it is they've come here for. A big duffel bag of cash would be nice, wouldn't it?"

"At least we know exactly where they are now," Mark said. "We should get a bit closer and see if we can spot them. What if they do decide to leg it over the fields?"

Jones looked skyward. "I suppose they might if they've spotted you pulling in. Which, let's face it, they probably have. Fine, let's see if we can sneak up on them."

Jones turned to the man with the clipboard and pointed. "If Finn Tinkler comes back this way then don't let him leave, understood?"

"Um. Why not?" the man asked.

Jones held his warrant card out towards him. "Because he's been a very naughty boy."

Mark led the three of them across the construction site. They did their best to stay hidden as they moved, which was easy enough given the number of obstacles between them and the finished homes, even if they did draw some strange looks from the builders they passed on the way.

They peered round from behind a parked skid loader.

"It could be any one of those houses," Mark said.

"Yeah, which is why it would have been better waiting for them to come out," his dad said. "We could still wait for them out here, I suppose."

As if hearing him, a few raindrops, cold and heavy, descended from the grey sky overhead.

"Great," Jones said.

Julia risked another peek round from their cover. "The door's open on that one," she murmured. "Should it be?"

Mark looked for himself. "No. They must be in there."

Jones gave him a nod. "Come on then."

They ran from the side of the loader crossing the twenty yards or so of newly laid street as the rain started to come down more heavily.

Jones led the way out but was soon outpaced by Mark who overtook him and made it to the ajar door first. He gently pushed it inwards and poked his head inside.

"I can't see anyone," he whispered to the others as they caught up.

Before Julia could reply, Mark had stepped into the building so she followed him in.

It was a spacious, detached house. Completely sterile at the moment, with the interior doors fitted and the walls painted but none of the fixtures in place.

Mark stepped through into the bare living room. There was a hole in the stud wall. By the looks of it, it had been hastily made with the hammer which now lay discarded on the floorboards. Bits of plasterboard had been knocked away exposing a cavity going up to about the height of Julia's knee, with plaster and flecks of paint littering the floor.

"That was my painting," Mark said glumly, looking at his feet.

"More importantly, what was in that hole?" Jones asked.

There was a muffled thud from somewhere else inside the house.

"Back door!" Jones called, and they rushed back out of the living room, almost colliding with one another in their haste, and ran as fast as they could through to the kitchen.

They were just in time to see someone disappearing out of the back door.

"Quick!" Julia shouted.

They followed their quarry out of the house into the bare earth that would become a back garden.

Ginny and Mr Tinkler were sprinting as fast as they could along the edge of the mud-splattered, white security fence which separated the site from the fields. Julia thought she could make out a break in the barrier further along. Mr Tinkler was holding something awkwardly in one hand as he ran, a sports bag perhaps.

"After them," Jones croaked, apparently admitting that his own chances of pursuit were slimmer than he was, and coming to a halt.

Julia and Mark didn't need to be told, they were already off and gaining on Ginny and Mr Tinkler.

Ginny was only making slow progress. Still in her heels, she would have struggled to run at the best of times. On the uneven ground, with the heels sinking in with every stride, she didn't stand a chance. She'd barely made it to the edge of the garden when Julia caught up with her.

With one final burst of speed, Julia launched herself forwards, handbag arcing out as she did so, and she clutched the back of Ginny's jacket in both hands and pulled her down to the ground.

She felt the woman move underneath her, trying to squirm away, but Julia pushed her weight down, such as it was, pinning Ginny to the floor. "No you don't," she said.

She could hear Jones approaching behind her.

Keeping her arms firmly on Ginny, Julia craned her neck to look up and was just in time to see Mark catching up with Mr Tinkler, a few feet before he reached the gap in the barrier.

Mark leapt, arms outstretched. Despite his build, he was never much of an athlete, Julia knew, and his attempt at a tackle failed.

He came crashing down into the dirt behind Mr Tinkler, but he did just manage to stretch an arm out and give Mr Tinkler's receding foot a tug. It was enough to throw him off his stride and he took one more long, stumbling step, his arms windmilling out to his sides, before he too came crashing down.

Both men struggled to recover but Mark was faster. With an ungainly but effective jump he flung himself on top of Mr Tinkler, relying on his body mass to push him down to the ground.

By now Jones had caught up to Julia and she allowed herself to slide sideways off from Ginny while the detective applied the cuffs to her slender wrists.

Without a word to her, Jones began slowly but determinedly to run after Mark and Mr Tinkler. Julia hurried along keeping pace with him.

Jones reached them and looked down at the two men on the ground, Mr Tinkler making a token effort to struggle.

"I've only the one pair of cuffs," Jones managed to say. "Think you can keep him there until help arrives?"

"With pleasure," Mark said, leaning forward on his captive.

"I'm not going anywhere, let me up," Mr Tinkler protested.

"I think we're all right for now," Mark said. It was good that he wasn't taking any chances, but Julia couldn't help feeling that he was enjoying himself as well.

Jones stooped down to pick up the black leather sports bag which had slipped from Mr Tinkler's hand as he fell. Julia peered over his shoulder as he unzipped it.

There were stacks of fifty-pound notes, enough to stuff the bag to the brim.

Jones gave out a low whistle. "Here is our embezzled money, then," he said, zipping it back up again.

Very briefly, a thought flitted through Julia's head. Just how long would that money keep the bookshop afloat for?

She forced the thought away and turned to look in the other direction, away from temptation and through the gap in the security fence.

She gave a gasp and started running again, hopping over Mr Tinkler's prone head as she beelined for the fence.

"Julia? What is it?" Mark shouted to her as she went.

She didn't stop but called back. "Just keep him still!"

The gap wasn't that much wider than her, Mr Tinkler would have struggled with it, but she squeezed through ignoring the snagged button on her coat as she went.

She was in the fields now, in the long grass, the ground underfoot springy and bumpy, and slippery with the fresh rain, but she forced herself on.

Perhaps she should have tried sneaking up a bit closer before she ran. Obviously her PI skills still needed some honing.

But she'd made her choice now and she committed to it, lungs burning as she ran single-mindedly across the field towards her quarry.

Julia wasn't making any ground, but she knew that she didn't need to. As they reached the edge of the field the long cutting of a rhyne appeared before them and her quarry came to a skittering halt, not sure what to do.

Julia closed the last few paces and reached down, looping two fingers under the dog's collar before she could get away again.

Breathless, Julia patted the collie gently on the head. "Good girl," she said.

Ever diligent, Julia checked the tag on the thin red collar. Definitely Queen Beanie.

"Let's get you back where you belong," Julia said, and leaning awkwardly over sideways she led the way back across the field to the construction site.

Already Julia could hear the sound of sirens coming from the direction of King's Barrow.

Chapter 19

Julia lifted the styrofoam cup to her lips and took a sip of the lukewarm liquid within. It was either tea or coffee, Julia wasn't sure. Whichever one it was, the police station seriously needed to upgrade their vending machine.

The door of the interview room opened and the top half of the police sergeant appeared around the frame of the door.

"I think we're all done with you, Miss Ford," the sergeant said.

Gratefully, Julia rose from her chair and left the interview room which she'd been in for a few hours now. She finished the last of the drink before leaving. She hoped it was coffee, as she was running on fumes at this point.

Mark was waiting for her in the corridor, sitting slumped on one of the uncomfortable little chairs that lined the wall. He was splattered all over in dried mud, as was Julia herself.

He rose as Julia approached and gave her a quick hug.

"Let's get out of here," Julia said, and arm in arm and covered in mud the two of them began a weary shuffle down the hall.

Just before they reached the reception area DI Freiland appeared next to them, Julia wasn't entirely sure where from.

Despite the culprits all but being handed to her on a silver platter, Freiland didn't look happy. Perhaps she never did. She stood in front of them blocking the way out.

"Ah, it's my two amateur sleuths," she said.

Freiland had spent plenty of time with both of them in the interview rooms, but she'd stuck strictly to taking down the facts. This seemed more personal somehow.

Julia didn't have the energy left to manage a smile and just stood blinking.

"I won't pretend that I'm happy about having outside investigators poking about in my case," Freiland said. From the flinty expression on her face Julia could well believe that. "However I'm sure Mr Cutty will be pleased that you've resolved this."

This seemed about as close to an apology as Julia was going to get from the woman so she mumbled a thank you. "Where is Mr Cutty anyway?" Julia asked. "Has he been released?"

Freiland gave a shrug as though the whole thing was completely immaterial. "I believe they started processing him out when you brought Miss Stroup and Mr Tinkler in," she replied.

That appeared to conclude the conversation because DI Freiland stepped aside and Julia and Mark made their way through the reception area and out into the late afternoon sunlight.

Just as they were descending the steps to the pavement, a car blasted its horn nearby. With her nerves already frayed, Julia jumped into the air. But as she turned to look she saw Ronald's car parked up on the double yellow lines just down the road, with Ronald hanging out of the driver's side window.

He looked even more tired than Julia did. And even in the short time of his incarceration it seemed that he'd lost weight and his suit was hanging slightly loose.

In spite of all this he wore a cheerful smile on his face and he was beckoning them over to him, a heavy gold watch sliding up and down his wrist as he waved his hand.

"They've finally let you out," he said.

"Well you're one to talk," said Mark.

The man's smile broadened. "Why don't you two jump in? I can give you a ride back to Biddle Rhyne."

"That's fine, I've got the van parked round the corner," Mark replied.

"Sure, sure," said Ronald. He looked at each of them in turn. "Obviously, I cannot thank you enough. You've kept me out of prison and by the sound of it you've saved my business too. I made the right call coming to you."

Julia felt herself blushing. "Well, you're very welcome," she said.

Ronald tapped the outside of his car door with his fingers. "Anyway, I realize that we've never discussed a fee."

Julia thought for a second before answering. "I don't need a fee, Ronald. I'm just glad I could help."

There were some strained noises coming from Mark beside her but she gently prodded him with her elbow and he shut up.

Ronald looked her in the eye. "Are you sure, Julia?"

"Positive."

He kept drumming thoughtfully on his car door. "Well, in that case I'll have to make sure that I become a regular shopper at my local bookshop," he said. "I'll have to clear some time to read, I feel like there's a big purchase coming on."

Julia smiled at him. Not that one loyal customer was going to keep the store afloat but it couldn't hurt. "I'll look forward to seeing you then," she said.

Ronald gave a wave and then retracted his hand into the car and revved the engine. "Take care," he called as he pulled off down the road.

* * *

They had a stop to make before they arrived at Biddle Rhyne. Mark's van pulled up in the courtyard outside Mr Moore's home. The sun was out, but a few puddles here and there still gleamed in patches.

The door of Mr Moore's studio banged open and he came flying out towards them. But unlike their first visit, he had a crooked smile on his face and his eyes twinkled. He held his hands out wide in greeting as they hopped down from the van.

"It worked then?" he called loudly to them as he hurried over.

"Yes it did," Julia said. "Ginny bought it hook, line, and sinker."

"What can I say?" said Mr Moore, pushing his hair back from his eyes. "I'm good at what I do."

"Yes you are," Julia said.

"I have to admit, it feels nice to use my talents for something beyond flogging products for companies," he said. "My Photoshops helping put away a killer. Who would have thought it, eh?"

"Yes, those two should be going away for a decent stretch," Mark said. "And with the money recovered, hopefully it will be making its way back to you soon enough."

Mr Moore's expression darkened, but only slightly. "Hm, yes, sadly they didn't just let me take my share out of the bag of cash they recovered," he said.

He clapped them both warmly on the shoulders. "Anyway, I have work to be doing and I should get back to the studio. But if your detective agency needs any help again just let me know, I'd be happy to oblige."

Julia and Mark bade him farewell and clambered back into the van. Julia hadn't felt the need to correct him about the detective agency, which she was still adamant didn't exist except inside Mark's head.

As Mark pulled the van around in a tight circle Julia let her head fall back against the headrest. "Speaking of work to do, that's a whole day at the shop gone," she said.

Mark made a dismissive noise and pulled out onto the lane. "The shop will survive," he said.

"Probably," Julia muttered.

"Home then?" Mark asked as the hedgerows sped past on either side, the tips of the branches brushing the van noisily as they went.

"You know what," said Julia. "How about the Barley Mow instead? I think we've earned it."

Mark smiled. "I'd say that we have, yes."

* * *

The old coaching inn was glowing in the afternoon light, the sun shining straight on to it over the flat expanse of moorland. The wind had picked up, setting the thick iron chain that cordoned the pub off from the road swaying. Overhead, the colourful pub sign creaked with each gust.

Julia pushed down the latch on the door to the parlour and stepped inside, Mark dipping his head to follow her in.

A couple sat at one of the tables on the side of the room, sipping drinks. They were dressed for walking and had some mud spattered on their trousers, but nothing to the extent that Julia and Mark had. The couple stared at them as they crossed the room.

Julia ignored them and stepped up to the bar. The bunting had come down now, and was lying in a sorry-looking pile next to the beer taps.

Behind the bar, Ivan gave a warm smile as they approached.

"Ah, I hear congratulations are in order," he said, his rich voice filling the small room.

Julia shared a look with Mark. "I guess they are," she said.

"Your first case solved, even if they did give you a run for your money by the looks of it." Ivan looked Julia's filthy clothes up and down.

She knew better than to wait for the offer of a free drink.

"And a £25 reward to boot, no wonder you're treating yourselves," Ivan continued.

It took Julia a moment to work out what Ivan was talking about. How he had heard about them finding the missing dog but not apprehending Beatrice Campbell's killers, she did not know.

Evidently when Sally was not working, his gossip game was low.

With her last reserves of strength, Julia climbed up onto one of the stools and leaned forward on the bar. Mark clambered onto the one beside her.

"A house red, please," Julia said.

Ivan huffed indignantly. "And I thought you were pushing the boat out," he said as he collected a wine glass from overhead. "Still, it's nice for me to have the company, I suppose."

Julia slid the glass across the bar and lifted it to her lips. It might only be the house wine but after the police station's attempt at a beverage it tasted like nectar. "Yes, you'll miss us when you're gone," Julia said.

Ivan made a harrumphing sound as he poured Mark's drink. "It doesn't look that way," he muttered.

"You won't miss us?" Julia said, affecting hurt.

"No, I mean the deal looks like it might fall through. Apparently the developer backing it was caught up in some dodgy accounting or something. The sale doesn't look like it will happen after all."

Julia looked around the ancient walls of the pub. She had her own share of history here too. Playing darts in order to impress the boys, or one boy in particular. Celebrating and commiserating with Sally, which seemed to happen in almost equal measure.

And of course there was the whole chain of events starting with the major's missing car which had led her to where she was now. Sitting next to Mark, running a struggling bookshop, and apparently an ad hoc detective agency as well.

She'd be lying if she said she wasn't pleased to see the old place preserved. But all the same she felt some sympathy for Ivan. She knew he put his heart and soul into the place, and only the dwindling income had prompted him to take up the offer to buy the pub.

She leaned forward and patted Ivan's hand gently. He raised an eyebrow at her questioningly.

"I'm sorry, Ivan," she said. "I know you were looking for your out."

Ivan waved it away. "Ah, never mind. The work here's all right and I'm sure I can muddle through for the time being."

Julia took another sip of wine and then swilled the remaining liquid around in the glass.

"Yes, I'm sure that's true," she said.

Acknowledgements

It's my pleasure to thank JP Weaver, Kendall Olsen-Maier, MachineCapybara, Caitlin L. Strauss, Delilah Waan, and Stuart Watkins for all of their help with this book.

And I'd like to thank again my wife and my dad for their support, and especially my mum, for her help with proofreading.

Finally, I'd like to thank everyone at The Book Folks, especially Polly and Tarek for their hard work.

If you enjoyed this book, please let others know by leaving a quick review on Amazon. Also, if you spot anything untoward in the paperback, get in touch. We strive for the best quality and appreciate reader feedback.

editor@thebookfolks.com

www.thebookfolks.com

More fiction in this series

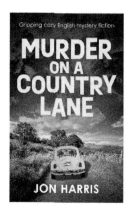

MURDER ON A COUNTRY LANE (Book 1)

After the shock of discovering a murder victim, young barmaid Julia isn't too perturbed because local garden centre owner Audrey White was a horrible so-and-so. But when her fingerprints are found all over a death threat, Julia becomes the police's prime suspect. Equipped with an unfetching ankle tag she must solve the crime to prove her innocence.

FREE with Kindle Unlimited and available in paperback!

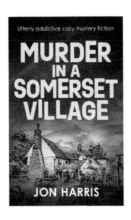

MURDER IN A SOMERSET VILLAGE (Book 2)

Julia has accomplished her dream of opening a bookshop!
Well, almost. It still needs refurbishing, and there are some
tricky planning laws to get around. But small beer! Yet she
is stopped in her tracks when tragedy strikes once more.
Someone is digging up the past in Biddle Rhyne, and
sticking knives into people's backs. Quite literally,
unfortunately…

FREE with Kindle Unlimited and available in paperback!

Other titles of interest

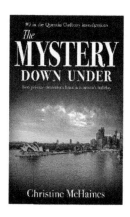

THE MYSTERY DOWN UNDER
by Christine McHaines

Evading a London gangster with a bone to pick, private investigator Quentin Cadbury and his sidekick Wanda Merrydrew decide to visit Australia to catch up with Quentin's family. Yet when they discover a burglar is causing upset in their quiet Sydney suburb, they can't help but get involved. Can Quentin catch a thief and prove his mettle to his ever-disappointed father?

FREE with Kindle Unlimited and available in paperback!

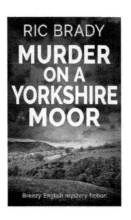

MURDER ON A YORKSHIRE MOOR
by Ric Brady

Ex-detective Henry Ward is settling awkwardly into
retirement in a quiet corner of Yorkshire when during a
walk on the moor he stumbles upon the body of a young
man. Suspecting foul play and somewhat relishing the
return to a bit of detective work, he resolves to find out
who killed him. But will the local force appreciate him
sticking his nose in?

FREE with Kindle Unlimited and available in paperback!

Sign up to our mailing list to find out about new releases and special offers!

www.thebookfolks.com